陶維極——著
G B Talovich

What an astonishing thing a book is.

It's a flat object made from a tree with flexible parts

on which are imprinted lots of funny dark squiggles.

But one glance at it and you're inside the mind of

another person,

maybe somebody dead for thousands of years.

Across the millennia, an author is speaking clearly and

silently inside your head,

directly to you.

Writing is perhaps the greatest of human inventions,

binding together people who never knew each other,

citizens of distant epochs.

Books break the shackles of time.

A book is proof that humans are capable

of working magic.

天文學家／ Carl Sagan

TABLE OF CONTENTS

Lesson III 高階語法與應用

Lesson IV 道地英文寫作訣竅

Lesson V 階段式實作練習

Lesson VI 實用範例說明

LET THE MAGIC BEGIN ▶ 前言

寫作是幻術：筆在紙上畫一畫、手指敲一敲鍵盤，千里外、百年後的人看到，了解你的想法，甚至喜怒哀樂，隨作者指揮。幾千年前，死亡的人又可以說話了。這不是幻術是甚麼呢？

寫作，傳達訊息；如果沒訊息要傳達，就不寫。但要傳達清楚的訊息讓讀者明白，不容易，特別是英文的表達畢竟和中文不同。

洋猩是我，陶維極，G B Talovich，美國人。十八歲來臺學中文，臺灣師大國文學、碩士，讀的是國文、本行是武術，可是為了養肚皮，教英文。已經教了幾十年了。為何要寫這本書呢？因為我意見很多。我看到版權代理、翻譯的英文寫作書，作者不了解華人寫作的特色（困難）；華人寫的，要嘛太過于古典文學，要嘛用中文寫作概念寫英文；這兩種的寫作風格都停留在十九世紀。

無論中外，我看到的寫作書都很悶、正經八百、了無生氣。好像要寫作，必須穿西裝打領帶、沐浴齋戒、正襟危坐、不苟言笑，萬一頭髮沒梳好就不允許撰文，而且都要寫些經綸濟世的崇高理想，寫的越艱澀、詞彙越冷僻，越厲害。教寫作不必要趣味，可是一定要那麼悶嗎？

寫作的功能，包羅萬象，但不論寫讀書心得、客服投訴、學術報告、情書、歷史研究、自傳，基本寫作要素不變。本書重點在于寫作技術，會寫了，無往不利。

提醒大家，寫作更沒辦法速成，一字要訣，就是：revise。無它，寫完，修改，修改完，重寫，重寫完，修改。要多多練習，所以本書有很多習題、參考例句。偶爾靈感來，下筆成文，可遇不可求。

要練習，可以把字句抄寫在電腦，慢慢修改。NEVER write English in a Chinese font! 打電腦寫 abc 的玩意，千萬不要用中文字型的 abc，因為間隔不對。選漂亮的字型（請參考 Chapter 13，字型心理學）；Times New Roman 很呆板、陳舊，還是請讀者考慮選其它字型。本猩選 Lexend Deca 排版，因為此字型易讀美觀，網路上可免費下載使用。

本猩推薦以「手抄」練習；練習時，一字一句抄在紙上，更有感覺；也推薦用 fountain pen 墨水筆，寫作更能享受。

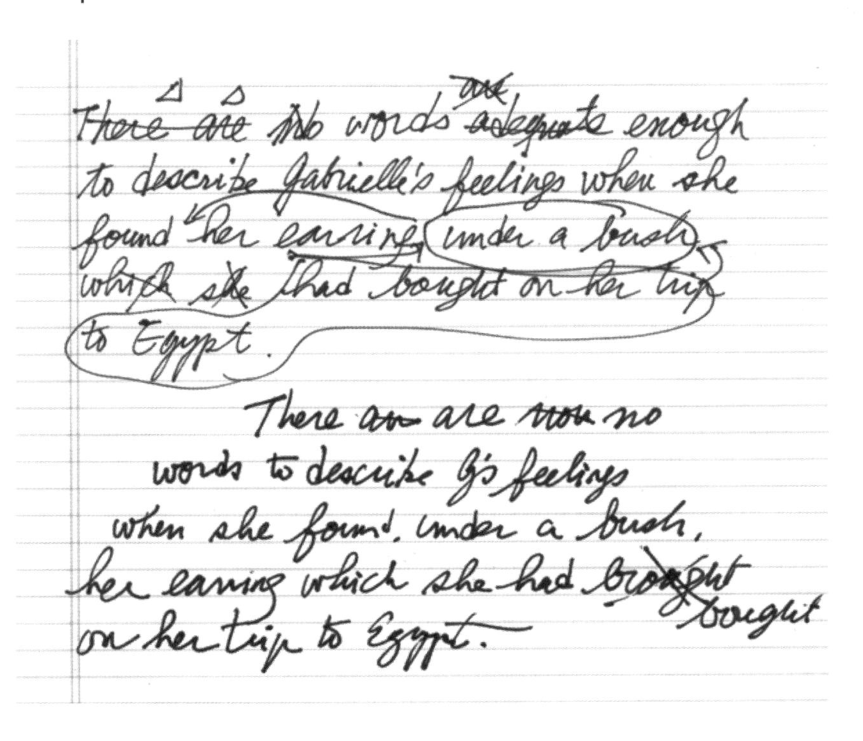

讀者手上這本書，我寫的很開心，希望各位讀了也能有收穫。

HOW TO USE THIS BOOK ► 如何使用本書

華人寫英語，往往短句居多，但英文慣用complex sentences。行文需節奏，該怎麼練，本書題庫練習可分三大類與漸進式寫作，正確用法採Lexend Deca字型示意，錯誤示範改用Times New Roman，方便大家辨識。

1. Combine these words into sentences.

將字串成句，盡量精簡順暢，同時注意時態、動詞、單複數、標點。

2. Combine these sentences.

將句子再組成、精煉好句。

3. Improve these sentences.

出拙句，大刀闊斧修改，力求通順文雅。先刪贅字！注意動詞、單複數等。同件事，本書提供不同寫法，可比較箇中差異。

4. Practice Writing

漸進式寫作練習，能寫多少就寫多少。

· **Complete these sentences.**
填格子，發揮想像力，替未完成的句子寫出各種可能。

· **Write a sentence for each of these words.**
就是造句。但請先確認每個字現在的正確語意、詞性，才能造好句。

· **Write an essay**
根據主題情境設定，換你來自由發揮寫文章。

練習示範說明

每章節根據主題需求，提供不同類型練習題庫。

Improve these sentences.

❶ She ran passed us without stop and say hello due to the fact that her bus about to pull out.

修改參考，歡迎舉一反三。

改：**She ran past us without stopping to say hello because her bus was about to pull out.**

評：Passed 是 pass 的過去式、過去分詞； past 是介系詞。Due to the fact that，囉唆：改 because。若寫 due to her bus being about to pull out，尚通，可是不是很漂亮。

主流英文應用語法與字詞分析，增加活用性。

可以找同學、朋友一起練習。寫完後，交換修改、批評。修改，可以狠，但說話要婉轉。因為寫作、修改、切磋，難免有情緒，所以本猩建議為家庭和諧，還是別找親人切磋。請讀者不要為這本書吵架。

[Take your time with this book.
Don't hurry.]

▶ 看看陶老師的 YouTube
頻道：【洋猩英文學堂】

Lesson I
寫作基本原則

Chapter 01 決勝關鍵：刪贅字

文筆要進步，第一招，也是最重要的一招，就是：刪贅字 **Omit needless words.**

由 Strunk and White 著的英文寫作寶典 *The Elements of Style*，此書當勤讀， 其中精要在于：機器沒有多餘的零件，文章沒有多餘的字。

Omit needless words. Vigorous writing is concise. A sentence should contain no unnecessary words, a paragraph no unnecessary sentences, for the same reason that a drawing should have no unnecessary lines and a machine no unnecessary parts.

如果刪字而文句猶可通，心不怕手不軟，刪！贅，就是罪。

贅字何罪？

買鞋子，鞋店如果賣三隻，我們一般人只有兩隻腳，你願意買三隻嗎？同理，三個字可以表達的，用五個字，就是多餘的。鞋子太大、太小，都不恰當。要剛剛好。文章也一樣。

寫文章，目的是要表達意思，如果不表達，就不寫。文句剛剛好，不多不少；怎麼拿捏，這就是功夫。所以孔子說，辭達而已矣。剛剛恰當，不多不少的意思。

老子注：行之無當曰贅。贅字，就是不當。而贅字顯現作者邏輯不緊湊、寫作的人沒想好。

例如，previous experience；experience 的定義，是經歷過的事，沒有未來的經驗，所以 previous 贅。刪！
倒過來，future plans：計畫，必定是未來的，future 贅。刪！可刪就刪！

贅字，也受母語影響。英語背景的人講華語，常出現「我是忙」之類的句型，受母語 be 動詞影響。華語背景的人寫英文，有的贅字受中文句型影響。

中文可以寫：因為他遲到了，所以電影頭五分鐘沒看到。
若寫英文：
Because he was late, therefore he missed the first five minutes of the movie，重複。要嘛 Because he was late, he missed the first five minutes of the movie，不然 He was late, so he missed the first five minutes of the movie，但兩者不可並存。

以文章的內容，therefore 太正式。若要強調文筆，不是用個 therefore 就算厲害了。Being late, he missed the first five minutes of the movie. 炫吧！

我們來看看幾個例句。

My friend she brought a kind of flower to put in the company.

改：**My friend brought a flower to put in the office.**

評：主詞是 my friend，不可贅加第二主詞 she。A kind of 表示某一種類別，不等于中文量詞「一種」；例如，A carnation is a kind of flower。Company 指公司、企業法人，而白領階級具體上班的場所是 office。

Due to the fact that there is a typhoon nearby in the vicinity, the event which was scheduled for tomorrow will hereby be called off. We hope to gather herbs together when the typhoon has moved elsewhere.

改：**There is a typhoon nearby, so the event scheduled for tomorrow will be called off. We hope to gather herbs when the typhoon has gone.**

評：Due to the fact that 囉唆，改 because。但勿常用 because 開句。Nearby 就是 in the vicinity。The event scheduled for tomorrow 也可寫 tomorrow's event。我們不是十八世紀的皇宮官僚，寫 hereby 幹嘛？ Gather 勢必 together，刪；除非 together 修飾 we，仍嫌語意不明。

My neighbor gifted me with a free gift, and that gift was an unexpected surprise.

改：**My neighbor surprised me with a gift.**

評：時下有人將 gift 當動詞，可吐。動詞用 give。Gift 是禮物，如果收費，不是禮物，所以刪 free。如果意料到，不是 surprise，刪 unexpected。

During the course of the boss's talk, we all had a feeling of sleepiness.

改：**During the boss's talk, we all felt sleepy.**

評：During 夠了，the course of 贅，刪。

In the court of law, the police officer gave a verbal account of the automobile accident, recounting the visual observations he made at the scene of the automobile accident.

改：**In court, the police officer described the automobile accident, recounting what he saw.**
In court, the police officer described the automobile accident, recounting what he had seen.

評：警察出庭，一定是法庭，不必贅述；難道是朝廷不成？英文「說」字多，speak about, tell about, say what happened, discuss, explain, 甚至 talk about，都很好，最不漂亮的、最做作的是 give a verbal account；visual observation 也做作：see, observe, witness 都比 make a visual observation 好。
不要把讀者當笨蛋；前半句已說明車禍，後半句不要重複。
不妨用過去完成式，明確說明前後順序。（past perfect，請參考 Chapter 8。）

去蕪存菁固然重要，
但要記得存菁！

Improve these sentences

❶ He placed the white color cup on the yellow colored mat which had a round shape, and at that point in time answered the question in a very convincing manner to the manager who was asking him.

❷ She loudly shouted for her dog because her dog was running along the left hand side of the street, chasing after a squirrel which was very, very large in size and wouldn't return back.

❸ Although electric cars are still few in number, experts tend to predict that in the foreseeable future, they will increase in number and become more popular, but in the meantime, the supply is adequate enough in order to meet the demand for them.

❹ They purchased marking pens in many different colors for the purpose of marking each separate group's respective materials.

❺ He was very, very mad when he dropped his camera which he had just bought down on the top of the table which was made of marble, because it was an import from a foreign country and it might get broken very easily and besides he paid a lot of money for it, too.

❻ In their opinion, many Korean people commonly believe that leaving a fan on while you sleep can lethally kill you dead.

參考例句

❶ **He placed the white cup on the round yellow mat, and then answered the manager convincingly.**

評：White、yellow 本是顏色，刪 color。Round 本來就是 shape。At that point in time，冗，then。經理沒問，不需要回答，刪 who was asking him。

❷ **She shouted for her dog because it was running along the left side of the street chasing a huge squirrel and wouldn't return.**

評：Shout 就大聲，不可能小聲 shout。back 冗，刪。

❸ **Although there are still few electric cars, experts predict that before long they will gain popularity, but in the meantime, the supply meets the demand.**

評：Few 是數量，刪 in number。英文的現在式涵蓋例外的可能，通常 tend to 可刪。

如果寫 Experts predict that although electric cars are still uncommon, they will eventually become more popular，又是 predict 又是 still uncommon，句型雖簡潔，但語意嫌前後抵觸。Adequate 等于 enough，刪一；the supply is adequate to meet the demand。乾脆刪二：the supply meets the demand. In order to，冗，刪 in order。

❹ **They bought marking pens in many colors to mark each group's materials.**

評：Many colors 必然是 different colors，刪；或可改為 marking pens in various colors。For the purpose of Ving，冗：to V。Each group 即可，刪 separate。刪 respective。

❺ **He was furious when he dropped his new camera on the marble table, because it was an import and very fragile, not to mention expensive.**

評：除非在太空站，drop 勢必 down：刪。掉落，勢必在桌面上，刪 on the top of。Import 本是從外國進口的，否則不是 import。

❻ **Many Koreans believe that leaving a fan on while you sleep can kill you.**

評：人家相信，當然是他們的意見：in their opinion 冗，刪。很多人有這種看法，自然是 common，刪。Kill，殺死，刪 lethally、dead 二字：的確我們要殺死贅字。

> The reader's first and simplest test of an author will be to look for words that do not function.
>
> 詩人／ Ezra Pound

Practice Writing

Complete these sentences. Use your imagination, tell stories, write as much as you wish, but make it interesting.

When he realized he had left his cellphone in the restaurant, _______

After the birth of their second child, _______

Three kilometers off the coast, the whale _______

When you hear about _______

After the game, there was always time to _______

Write a sentence for each of these words:

- notion
- obstinate
- integrity
- initiate
- condition

Write an essay.

Write about a friend who moved away or you have lost touch with. Describe how you met this person, what you liked about your friend (as well as what you may not have liked so much), what you did together, and anything else that comes to mind. Describe your friend's personality and looks. When and why did this person move or drift away? What else do you have to say?

美國開國元老 Ben Franklin 說了帽匠設計招牌的故事：

朋友甲來說，「廢話，看店就知道你做帽子 ，上面也畫帽子，hatter 可以刪。」好吧，把 hatter 塗掉了。

木匠路過，說，「For ready money」（十八世紀的用法，收現金，不賒帳，現在說 cash only 或 no credit），「我們這帶沒有人賒帳，不必寫。」有道理，刷子一揮，塗掉了三個字。

又一個朋友來，說，「帽子是誰做的，買的人不在乎，只要是好帽。」帽匠同意，把 makes and 刪除了。才刪掉了，刷子還沒放好，隔壁太太說，「當然是賣呀，難道你送帽子嗎？」帽匠點頭稱是，sells 立即刪。

村長看了，說，「本村的人都知道你是誰，外地來的客人，只要有帽子就好了，管你尊姓大名。」建議把 John Thompson 劃掉。

于是乎，帽匠發現招牌只剩：

Chapter 02 英文章法：餌大小結

中文標準佈局是「起承轉合」，英文標準佈局是「餌大小結」。

英文先放個餌，引起讀者興趣；寫大局；縮小範圍回到餌；總結。這是爬格匠千篇一律的寫法。寫中文一定要起承轉合嗎？寫八股文，一定要，否則斟酌。英文的餌大小結，一樣的道理。

英美老師很感冒的一種寫法，是華人喜歡寫的第一點如何如何、第二點如何如何等。偶用，可，但看起來像流水帳，沒有章法。

華人學英文，當然尋求成語，因為中文的成語是歷代讀書人留下的精華。殊不知，英文的 proverbs，往往是鄉下人留下的老調，不等于成語。

中文行文多引典故，常用成語，英文視為 clichés，通常忌諱。甚至英國文豪 George Orwell 建議，Never use a metaphor, simile, or other figure of speech which you are used to seeing in print. 尤其考托福，很多考生以為要加甚麼名人句，大可不必！甚至有人背幾句，不管題目，硬塞進去。若到美國課堂上這樣寫，小心老師甩椅子。

中文典故顯深度，但英文忌諱 **clichés**：陳腔濫調。

> 明、蘇伯衡討論文筆，說：
> 不在繁不在簡，狀情寫物在辭達。

英文常見 clichés，諸如 birds of a feather flock together, two heads are better than one, learn to walk before you run, make hay while the sun shines, every cloud has a silver lining 等等，不是絕不能用，但少用為妙，自己動動腦筋想，到底想要表達什麼？

要注意：很多臺灣編的英文教材教的 clichés，本猩從來沒看過，也看不懂，如 Homer sometimes nods、money makes the mare go，不知所云，更不鼓勵使用。

今天吃晚餐，要用刀叉？筷子？

刀叉、筷子，沒有對錯，沒有好壞，不一樣而已。請勿問，中文好？英文好？不一樣，沒有勝負。

Cliché 定律

甚麼是 cliché ？不用大腦，自動植入的字句、情景。例如從前臺灣連續劇一定要一幕：「媽媽！妳不能死！」「太太！我對不起妳！」

後來的 cliché，男主角高富帥，女主角美若天仙、家產萬貫、一頭烏溜溜的長髮、愛彈鋼琴，男主角與女友生口角，深夜一定要下雨，路上沒人，只見男主角一人在雨中垂頭喪氣走，突然女友伸出手，為男主角撐傘。觀眾搖頭：又來這套！

Practice Writing

Complete these sentences. Use your imagination. Try not to write something obvious. Think a bit.

When the credit card bill arrived, ________________

To restore order in the kindergarten, the teacher ________________

Six potatoes ________________

The groom ________________

The wedding ring ________________

Write a sentence for each of these words.

- whinnied
- mishap
- deadlock
- slouch
- aspect

Write an Essay.

Write about some historical figure. When and where did this person live? What did this person do? How has this affected your life (if at all)? Why did you choose this person?

Chapter 03 內容架構：5W1H

「我不知道怎麼寫！」看到題目，寫不出來。想不出寫甚麼。怎麼辦？對不起，本書已出售，不可退還，所以還是要寫。

首先，看到題目，敘述概況。由小而大，由大而小，均可。要寫多詳細？例如，假設題目是「欒樹」，要形容長相？利用價值？生長環境？觸及的回憶？先決定方向，然後想，怎麼取捨？

美國記者、小學生作文的訓練，要交代 **5 Ws: who, what, why, when, where**，再加 **how**。

其次，寫收穫、感觸、感想、心得。起頭寫的概況，連結到你自己的經驗、技術、知識。能不能延伸？記住焦點，不要離題。

再來，探索、解釋、追溯。探究原因、動機、狀況、基本議題，與表面現象的關聯、影響、牽扯。

重點：順序不拘。

結尾，依據探索得到的更深一層的結論、結尾、結局、壓軸戲。意義何在？不需要寫 in conclusion、to summarize。寫出來的結論、結尾，假使讀者看不出是結局，證明寫的太弱：重來。本猩曾經說過寫作很簡單嗎？沒有。重來。

如筏喻者，
法尚應捨，何況非法。

Bossy and the Train

從前，美國小鎮都有自己的報社，報導地方新聞。一年輕人想當記者，所以從小地方小報開始。他第一次跑新聞，報導農夫穀倉燒毀，他寫 A farmer's barn burned to the ground.

寫了一句，不知道後面該怎麼鋪陳，主編罵："Didn't anybody teach you the Five Ws and an H? What! Why! When! Who! Where! How!" 叫他下次一定要交代清楚，不然要走路了。

剛好過幾天，某農夫的乳牛走上鐵軌，被火車撞死：在農業區，這算重大事件，所以年輕記者採訪。回來寫的報導：

Four hundred fifty-six and a half yards northeast of the Dudley railroad crossing, the 2:15 St Paul & Pacific bound from the Ottumwa Junction to Coburg, with K. C. Jones (age 34) at the throttle, struck and killed a cow belonging to Josiah Cook (age 48). Her name was Bossy (age 5).

撰文，恰到好處。筷子需要兩根，恰恰好，多一根少一根、太長太短，都不行。

Chapter 04 文章脈絡：製造故事高潮起伏

請比較以下三篇文章：

Essay A

I'd like to visit Kalmykia because I think it is beautiful. I have never been there. I would like to go there. People live there. They have scenery. They have weather. They have culture. They have animals. So I would like to visit Kalmykia.

Essay B

I would like to visit the nation of Kalmykia, officially known in English as the Republic of Kalmykia (Хальмг Таңһч in Kalmyk, and Республика Калмыкия in Russian). This nation, with a population of 289,481 as recorded in the 2010 census, is located directly north of the North Caucasus. The capital, Elista, is located at the latitude 46° 18' 28" North and longitude 44° 15' 20" East. The northernmost point of the country is in Maloderbetovsky district, at a latitude of 48° 27' 12.82" North. The easternmost point is in Limansky district, latitude 47° 51' 74.83" East, and the westernmost point is in Salsky district, latitude 41° 63' 97.97" East. Kalmyikia reaches as far south as 44° 75' 99.01" North. The capital sits at an elevation of 133 meters above sea level and so on and so forth for another 28 pages.

Essay C

Kalmykia is the only Buddhist nation in Europe. The people don’t look like most Europeans. That is because the ancestors of the Kalmyks migrated from Siberia about four hundred years ago.

Kalmykia is scorching hot in the summer and freezing cold in the winter. The vast open grasslands are home to a very unusual animal called the saiga antelope. I would like to go to Kalmykia during their famous annual international chess championships to watch great chess players, visit the Buddhist temples and, if I have a chance, see some saiga antelopes.

哪一篇好看？為何？哪一篇讓讀者印象深刻？為何？
Essay A 雖短，而讀者已經開始死眉瞪眼、想逃無路，因為寫的每句空泛、籠統、沒有焦點。Essay A 每句可以形容天下每一個國家，太不 specific，抓不到讀者興趣。

本猩雖然強調 be specific，而 Essay B 太過于 specific；Essay C 恰到好處。怎麼拿捏，見作者功力。

寫作，傳達訊息，寫清楚，寫細節，寫重點，寫故事。要生動，不要死氣。

文章是案頭之山水
山水是地上之文章
清、張潮　幽夢影

Chapter 05 敘事節奏：短而有力

石碇山坡岩石掉落。大概是甚麼原因？

甲：黑衣人半夜搖動石塊，並在石後裝了遙控振動器，聯合國常任理事會決定時辰，請阿曼蘇丹國的蘇丹按鈕發動。

乙：隱居不老仙人練功，運氣撼動地下礦脈，震落此塊岩石。

丙：政府為了防止人民帶太多石頭回家，派人用三秒膠把石碇區山坡所有石頭黏住，而這塊沒黏好。

丁：下雨後，土壤鬆動，引力讓石頭滾落。

請問，讀者認為哪一種解釋最合理？若不選丁，本猩不知道該怎麼說呢。

且慢：為何選丁？因爲最近常理、附加條件最少。這符合 Occam's razor，修道士 William of Ockham (c1287 – 1347) 快刀，亦名 the law of parsimony，簡約法。簡單說，若許多說法可以解釋同一現象，最簡單的說法應該對。換言之，若無需要，不要增加條件：Entities should not be multiplied without necessity：我們來晾一下網路抄下的拉丁文：Non sunt multiplicanda entia sine necessitate.（炫吧！）能省則省，若無必要，勿增說詞。

若各說紛云，選附加條件最少的說法。
寫作同理。唯學術研究，盡量將簡單事情說得複雜。

他、她、它

現在強調男女平等，而 man、he 之類的詞似乎專指男性，不含女性，視為不尊重女性。

首先，man 確指男性，亦可指所有人，涵蓋女性，如 mankind。但因為有人嫌 man 似乎排除女性，所以改用 person。本猩喜歡 man 字，一則因為一音節，比 person 緊湊；再來因為 man 字根是思考，屬于日耳曼語，近英語；person 是舞台上的假面具，來自拉丁文。

代名詞怎麼辦？ He 是男性代名詞，也涵蓋女性。從前寫作，第三人稱很不假思索下 he，造成些荒謬的句例：The pregnant patient is to be taken to the ward where he is to be given a bed. 好奇特的生理！ The pregnant patient is to be taken to the ward where she is to be given a bed 就好了；稍嫌囉唆，可以更精簡：The pregnant patient is to be taken to the ward and given a bed.

為了避免這種 he，有人寫 he/she 或 s/he，還有 his/her、him/her， 缺點是版面不俐落，不漂亮。也有人乾脆用 they，可是 they 明明是複數，語法拐來扭去：The officer held the suspected murder weapon in their hand，到底幾位警察共用一隻手？

性別多元，所以往往有人在名字後注明慣用的代名詞，如：
Lauren: they, their
若是這樣，就尊重，照他們的習慣用。

如果選擇代名詞不安，就避開：

Each passenger should put his carry-on luggage into the overhead compartment. 女乘客怎麼辦？

Each passenger should put his or her luggage into the overhead compartment. 拙 。

Each passenger should put their luggage into the overhead compartment. 是嗎？可是 each 是「每一」，而 their 是複數。算了吧：Luggage should be put in the overhead compartment. 被動語氣還是有它的妙用。

這個問題，我想給下一代的人處理，過五十年，塵埃落定看著辦。在我們目前尚未演變出共用代名詞，本猩往往用 he 涵蓋所有人，但需斟酌。

Lesson II
基礎文法與應用

Chapter 06 現在式：表述常態現象

基本型態：**S am/are/is adj/noun/** 介系詞片語
S V

所謂的「現在式」，通常表示一種狀況、一個常態，目前如此，從前這樣，將來也大概如此；例如，I know where Belgrade is. 我很久以前知道貝爾格勒在哪，我現在知道，我將來也應該會知道；我的認知不變、貝爾格勒的位置不變，所以用現在式。

Be 動詞的現在式，時間範圍可能比較短，例如 I am busy：我在忙。但一樣可以表示常態：Rita is an occupational therapist.

除了 be 動詞，英文的現在式，並不一定現在正在發生。He works in the post office，並不表示他現在正在上班，而是說明他的工作。如果正在發生，就要用進行式。

本書不是文法課本，但華人學英文普遍有共同障礙。華語沒有動詞時態，所以華語背景的人寫英文，往往一概都用現在式：💣 My grandfather lives in Taipei and he works in a garages for thirty year and he dies four year ago（錯誤示範！）. 這當然不合英文的用法。應改為：My grandfather lived in Taipei and worked in a garage for thirty years. He died four years ago.

「他習慣穿牛仔褲上班，」華語背景的人義無反顧把這類句型譯：💣 He is used to wearing jeans to work. 但 be used to 意思是勉強適應、不得已才這樣。正確英語是：He wears jeans to work. 現在式表示常態，通常如此。

Combine these words into sentences.

Use no redundant words. Remember to punctuate.

1. he / mad / text / from boss / report / due / tomorrow
2. when / they / go / grocery store / buy / two / leaves / bread / fruit / vegetables / maybe / couple / packs / cookies

> 一般寫作不要用縮寫（contractions），除非是不正式、寫對白。寫 I am，不寫 I'm；寫 does not，不寫 doesn't。

3. usually / traffic jam / southbound / freeway / rush hour / especially / rain
4. sesame oil / refrigerator/ looked cloudy/ brought back / room temperature / returned to normal / tasted / good / before
5. pile / receipts / by / computer / you / initial / before / meeting / three / o'clock

> 全名如 John Fitzgerald Kennedy，initials 取每字首字母：JFK。文件不需要正式簽名，但表示已閱，簽 initials 即可。于此 initial 可以當動詞。

參考例句

❶ **He is mad about the text from his boss about the report that is due tomorrow.**
He is mad about the text from the boss, because the report is due tomorrow.
He was mad about the text from the boss, because the report is due tomorrow.

評：若寫 he is mad，氣尚未消；若 he was mad，已消。假如寫 the report was due tomorrow，通常表示改期了，現在不需要明天交。區別 be mad about 事與 be mad at 人。

❷ **When they go to the grocery store, they buy two loaves of bread, some fruit, some vegetables, and maybe a couple packs of cookies.**
When they went to the grocery store, they bought two loaves of bread, some fruit and vegetables, and a couple of packs of cookies.

評：Some fruit and vegetables 尚可，但因為 fruit 不可數，與 vegetables（複數）互相連接有些不順。A couple of packs，可省為 a couple packs；a couple Ns 不定數，兩三個。

> Groceries 是菜，帶回家打算吃的東西叫做 groceries，並不是「雜貨」。我們要用廿一世紀的英文，不用十八世紀的英文。

注意：When they go to the grocery store, they buy groceries，依照此句寫法，他們常去買菜云云。寫 When they went to the grocery store, they bought groceries，過去某一次買了這些。

❸ **Usually, there is a traffic jam on the southbound freeway during the rush hour, especially when it rains.**
There is usually a traffic jam on the southbound freeway during the rush hour, especially if it rains / if there is rain.

評：並不表示現在塞車、下雨。

❹ **The sesame oil in the refrigerator looked cloudy, but when I brought it back to room temperature, it returned to normal, and tasted just as good as before.**
When the sesame oil was in the refrigerator it looked cloudy, but once it was brought back to room temperature, it returned to normal, and tasted just as good as before.

❺ **There is a pile of receipts by the computer for you to initial before the meeting at three o'clock.**
Initial the pile of receipts by the computer before the three o'clock meeting.

Combine these sentences.

❶ The boy is happy. He won a prize. He flew his kite very high. None of the other people could fly their kites so high.

❷ The Academy Awards ceremony was held as usual in 2022. It did not go smoothly because something bad happened. The ceremony was thrown into disorder for a few minutes. Chris Rock was the presenter. He made a joke. It was not very funny. Will Smith is an actor. He acts like a child. He heard the joke. He suddenly lost his temper. He abruptly went up on stage without permission. He gave the aforesaid Chris Rock a slap in the face.

❸ Cooking takes time. People do not have a lot of time in this day and age. People are always in a hurry. A microwave oven makes it simple to cook. It also makes it faster to cook. Therefore, most people think that they have to have a microwave in their kitchen. They cannot do without their microwave.

❹ We want to play a game of volleyball. We have only 3 people. We can't play volleyball.

❺ Every morning she wakes up at 5. She practices yoga. She practices it in the living room. Nobody else in her family wakes up that early.

參考例句

❶ **The boy is happy about winning a prize for flying his kite higher than anybody else.**

評：比較級加 any、other、else ＝最高級。

❷ **The 2022 Academy Awards ceremony was disrupted when, in a childish fit of temper, the actor Will Smith barged on stage and slapped the presenter, Chris Rock, in the face over a lame joke.**

評：若寫 barged on stage to slap，文意稍異：想甩巴掌，但未必甩成了。不寫 aforesaid，文筆立馬進步。

❸ **Since they simplify and speed up cooking in today's rushed society, microwave ovens have become indispensable in modern kitchens.**
The pace of life is so fast that nowadays people do not have time to cook, so many think microwaves are essential because they simplify and speed up cooking.

評：一般人在廚房做餐點，所以可以不說明 kitchen。

❹ **There are not enough people to play a game of volleyball.**
There are only three of us, so we cannot play volleyball.
We do not have enough people to play a game of volleyball.
We need another nine people to play a game of volleyball.
We want to play a game of volleyball, but we are nine people short.

評：A game of 亦可省，除非強調只打一場排球。

❺ **Every morning before the rest of her family wakes up, she wakes up at 5 to practice yoga in the living room.**
Every morning, she wakes up at 5 to practice yoga in the living room before the rest of her family wakes up.
Every morning at 5, she wakes up to practice yoga in the living room before the rest of her family wakes up.
She wakes up every morning at 5 to practice yoga in the living room before the rest of her family wakes up.

> Short words are best and the old words when short are best of all.
>
> 英國首相／Winston Churchill

Improve these sentences.

1. The boy is so exciting for trip to zoo, because he is very like the animal there, especially the panda.

2. People say, but maybe this not true, but people say how coffee begins, it was in Ethiopia maybe a thousand years before, and a man his name Kaldi he have goat many goat and it have tree with berry and the goat eat berry and jump up and down and run back and forth and act crazy when they eat that berry, Kaldi see the berry is shiny and red.

3. There have many, many people buy ticket observe National Basketball Association (NBA) professional basketball player play competition game against the other team.

4. His parent are supportive of his avowed intended arrangement to pursue a further education in the field of visual graphic design.

5. “Demon Slayer: Kimetsu no Yaiba” is many people read manga and become anime and many people watch it tell about a boy his name“Kamado Tanjiro”, he is a teenager and a demon slaughter his family members and his sister “Nezuko” make demon so “Tanjiro” he want slay many many demon and to save her sister.

> Kimetsu no Yaiba, 鬼滅之刃；Kamado Tanjiro, 竈門炭治郎；Kamado Nezuko, 竈門禰豆子。

參考例句

❶ **The boy is excited about the trip to the zoo, because he likes the animals there a lot, especially the pandas.**

評：The trip is exciting, the boy is excited. Be like N，像；like N，喜歡。

如果動物園只有一隻熊貓，再來沒有其他動物，或此男只喜歡一隻熊貓，其它都不喜歡，才可以寫 animal、panda。否則要複數。

❷ **Legend traces the origin of coffee a thousand years to an Ethiopian goatherd named Kaldi who noticed that his goats frolicked after eating shiny red berries.**
Legend traces the origin of coffee a thousand years to Kaldi, an Ethiopian goatherd who noticed that his goats frolicked after eating shiny red berries.

評：加強字彙，文筆緊湊。注意單複數、時態。

Before、after 要注名時間定點之前後：a thousand years before，讀者自然問：before what?

一句一主詞：a man he have 變成兩個主詞。

❸ **Crowds of people buy tickets to watch NBA games.**

評：家喻戶曉 NBA，一般文章不必贅述。英文現在式沒有 there have 的句型！

❹ **His parents support his plan to learn more about graphic design.**

評：此句不知道 parent 是指父親或母親，或者父母雙親。
Be supportive of，三個字，囉唆，而 supportive 是形容詞，換動詞 support。

❺ **The popular manga and the following anime, *Demon Slayer: Kimetsu no Yaiba*, tell the story of a teenager named Kamado Tanjiro who toils to slay demons because a demon slaughtered his family, and to save his sister Nezuko, who was turned into a demon.**

評：作品名稱用斜體字，盡可能勿用引號。姓名首字大寫，不加引號。
引號多，版面凌亂，該避免。
此句 demon 出現四次，考慮寫 to slay demons because one slaughtered his family 或 to slay demons because his family was slaughtered by one。
若寫 who toils to save his sister Nezuko, who was turned into a demon, and to slay other demons because they slaughtered the rest of his family，句子簡潔，但題目是 *Demon Slayer*，所以重點應放在鬼，禰豆子次之。
引號正確用法，請參考 Chapter 11。

有的作家敘述故事用現在式，以為這樣比較生動、身歷其境，卻很容易時態錯亂、讓讀者厭煩。*Robert's Rules of Writing* 的作者 Robert Masello 說，I find the pretense precious and vaguely annoying，並指出用現在式寫作讓讀者與情景脫解、使故事緩慢。

英文的時態很美、很精準，好好發揮吧！當然要看寫作的類別：假如敘述科學定律、說明書，「現在式」最適合：

- Earth rotates around the sun. 這是常態，不轉還得了！
- The flashlight requires one 18650 rechargeable lithium-ion battery. 只要這款手電筒還在生產，這句就要用現在式。

所敘述的事情，理應有人、事、物、地、時、起因。寫的清楚才生動。

Practice Writing

Complete these sentences. Use your imagination.

The new residents hung the calendar on the wall and

____

She heard the voices of the choir ___________________

He got dressed quickly, putting on his best ___________________

The General Manager sat in his office like a king on his throne,

____

With devilish satisfaction, she ___________________

Write a sentence for each of these words.

You may want to look the words up to make sure you know how to use them.

- measures
- separate
- bland
- frustrated
- inaudible

Write an essay.

Put this fascinating book down for a moment, and look around. What do you see? Write about the place you are, right now. Describe what you see. Don't just write a list of the articles you see. Give details, tell a story. Pay attention to the structure of your essay.

Chapter 07 過去式：說明過去的人事物

基本型態：**S was/were adj/noun/** 介系詞片語
S Ved

過去式，表示事情已經過了，已經結束了。例如，He was here，表示他以前在這裏，但是現在不在。I forgot her name，表示我曾經忘記她的名字，可是我現在想起來了。

過去式另一種用法，表示當時的情形，與現在無關。例如，我講上個月的事情，說 I wasn't here，表示我當時不在場；至于我現在在哪，無關緊要。

Combine these words into sentences.

Use the past tense.

1. cat / startled / loud noise / you / dropped / pile / books
2. dark / living room / good photo
3. Beethoven made / breakfast / coffee / great / care / counting / precisely / sixty / beans
4. Kevin / brought / wrong data / important / meeting / manager / upset
5. he / saw / mountain bike / wanted / buy / on sale / bicycle store / still expensive / arranged / boss / buy / time plan

Time plan，亦稱 installment plan，分期付款。一期的款項，叫做 installment.

參考例句

❶ **The cat was startled by the loud noise you made when you dropped that pile of books.**
The cat was startled by the loud noise when you dropped the pile of books.

評：例句著眼點在貓，所以用被動。但撰文，被動句少用為妙。可以寫 The loud noise the pile of books you dropped made startled the cat 而重點移到書。寫 The loud noise you made when you dropped the pile of books startled the cat 責怪人粗心。

❷ **It was too dark in the living room to take a good photo.**

評：英文的 too 帶否定的意思：太過于 adj，所以無法 verb/noun。

❸ **Beethoven made his breakfast coffee with great care, counting out precisely sixty beans.**

❹ **Kevin brought the wrong data to the important meeting, so the manager was upset.**
The manager was upset that Kevin brought the wrong data to the important meeting.
The manager was upset because Kevin brought the wrong data to an important meeting.

評：亦可寫 Kevin brought the wrong data to the important meeting, which upset the manager.

❺ **He saw the mountain bike he wanted to buy on sale at the bicycle store, but it was still expensive, so he arranged with the boss to buy it on a time plan.**

Combine these sentences.

1. The manager was late to work. He didn't come to the office until 9:20, and the workday starts at 9:00. He comes to work on the bus. The bus was late. This happened on Wednesday.

2. Rodavan was confused. The questions on the test confused him. The test was about Statistics. He took the test yesterday.

3. Thomas Jefferson was the third President of the United States. He was the main author of the Declaration of Independence. Thomas Jefferson had a mansion. It was called Monticello. He grew sesame there. He did that for the seeds. He pressed the seeds to get oil. He used the oil on salad.

4. Alexandra was on television. She was on a news report. The news report was at 7 o'clock last night. It was on Channel ABC. The news report was about a deer. The deer jumped into her chickenyard. She saw the deer jump into her chickenyard. She filmed it. The chickenyard is in back of her house.

5. Someone dropped a cigarette butt. Somebody was careless. The cigarette was still burning. It started a fire. A house burned to the ground. The insurance company estimated the damages. The fire destroyed a value of $100,000.

參考例句

1. **The manager was twenty minutes late to work on Wednesday because his bus was late.**
   Arriving at the office at 9:20 on Wednesday, the manager was twenty minutes late because his bus was late.

2. **Rodavan was confused by the questions on the Statistics test he took yesterday.**
   Rodavan was confused by the questions on yesterday's Statistics test.
   The questions on yesterday's Statistics test confused Rodavan.

評：第三句寫法，重點在題目，不在考生 Rodavan。

3. **The third President of the United States, Thomas Jefferson, the main author of the Declaration of Independence, grew sesame at his mansion, Monticello, to press salad oil from the seeds.**
   Thomas Jefferson, the main author of the Declaration of Independence and the third President of the United States, grew sesame at Monticello, his mansion, to press the seeds for salad oil.

❹ **Alexandra was on the 7 o'clock news on Channel ABC last night about a deer she filmed jumping into the chickenyard in back of her house.**
Alexandra was on last night's 7 o'clock news on Channel ABC about a deer she filmed jumping into the chickenyard behind her house.
Alexandra was on Channel ABC's 7 o'clock news last night because she filmed a deer jumping into the chickenyard in back of her house.

> on television，上電視；
> on the television，電視機上面。
> in back of 在～的後面，在外面；
> in the back of，在～的後面，在裏面。

❺ **A carelessly dropped burning cigarette butt started a fire that burned a house to the ground, causing damages estimated at $100,000.**
A burning cigarette butt, carelessly dropped, caused a fire that burned a house to the ground, with damages estimated at $100,000.
An unextinguished cigarette butt, careless discarded, started a fire that burned a house to the ground, resulting in damages estimated at $100,000.
A house burned to the ground in a fire started by a carelessly discarded, unextinguished cigarette butt, causing damages estimated at $100,000.

評：選哪一句，看前後文、節奏、重點。

Improve these sentences.

1. Him and his friend ran race because want to find out he the fastest or his friend the fastest.
2. After the presentation was totally finished, three people who join the audience ask multiple question
3. During the course of the meeting, the manager mentioned about the reduced number of sales which have been transacted during the period from June through and including August, and promulgated his requirement that the situation mentioned above must has to be ameliorated and mitigated.
4. The teacher redundantly repeated statements, saying statements which he had stated before in an earlier context.
5. Before Mr Hall travel by jet from Los Angeles and go to London, he park car parking garage not far from airport, have 250 lots in that parking garage.

參考例句

❶ **He and his friend ran a race to see who was faster.**

評：若寫「我」與「他人」，「我」應列後面；現在年輕人偶寫 me and my friends，不漂亮又自大。只有二人賽跑，用比較級，最高級需要三項以上。

❷ **After the presentation, three people in the audience asked many questions.**

評：完成就是完成，不必加 totally。甚至 after 已表示結束，可刪 finished。Join 是成為一員的過程；一則 audience 是烏合之眾，不需要揀選才能加入；二則如果 joined，未必目前還參加。Multiply 的意思是繁殖，引伸為九九乘法的乘，而基本上有「重複」的意味。時下有人喜歡將 multiple 當 many 的同義詞，做作：many 就 many。
嚴格說，multiple books 就是一種書的若干本；很多不同的書，樸素的 many books 反而對。

注意：時態、單複數、標點。

❸ **During the meeting, the manager pointed out the decline in sales from June through August, and said that the situation has to improve.**

評：During 涵蓋 the course of。Mention 是簡單提一下，與敘述的狀況不合；mention 直加受詞，不可加 about。如果寫 bring up，字意可以，但接著寫銷售量下降，又 up 又 down，不要把文章寫成雲霄飛車；選 pointed out。寫一般通用英文，寫 promulgate、ameliorate、mitigate 之類的古澀詞彙，讀者不會崇拜你。寫法律文件，「上文」可以寫 above，但口頭上沒有上下文；如果怕對方不了解，可以寫 the situation just mentioned、the situation just discussed，但大可不必。

❹ **The teacher repeated himself.**

❺ **Before flying from Los Angeles to London, Mr Hall parked his car near the airport in a parking garage with 250 spaces.**

評：Parked his car near the airport in a parking garage 不理想，但為了避開 airport 孤立在 spaces 後，只好這樣寫。但一句不要裝太多內容；parking garage 幾個車位，與 Hall 先生的旅行關係不大，應該可以刪除，句子就順了：Before flying from Los Angeles to London, Mr Hall parked his car in a parking garage near the airport. 甚至如果讀者應該知道他開的是汽車，或者交通工具不重要，可以逕寫 Mr Hall parked in a parking garage near the airport.

Garage 可當車庫亦可當修車廠。因為已說明停車，可刪除 parking。

parking space: 停車位
parking lot: 停車場

Practice Writing

Complete these sentences. Use your imagination. Don't bore your reader.

When I opened the new bar of soap, I realized ____________

She thought she knew him well until ____________________

The flood waters kept rising ____________________

Before he even saw it, the punch landed on his ________________

The police car ____

Write a sentence for each of these words.

- destitute
- complacent
- porcupine
- charm
- startled

Write an essay.

Write about what you did yesterday. Remember to use the past tense. Give details, tell a story. Don't be boring, don't be trite.

> 有人說，Good writing has a strong purpose. Bad writing has either no direction or has too many.

你寫的是中式英文還是道地英文？

最近看一篇中英翻譯範例，有一句：They are easy to make various mistakes. 💣這句「英文」純粹是中文：他們很容易犯各種錯。英文應該怎麼寫呢？They frequently make mistakes. 便了。如果硬要把「容易」譯出，勉強可以寫 It is easy for them to make mistakes，但犯錯本非難事。

為甚麼 various 不見了？因為英文有複數，除非要強調不是同一個錯一而再、再而三一直犯，不需要用 various，名詞加 s 就好了。妙吧！

還有一點要強調：凡是用電腦寫 abc，一定要用英文字型，千萬不可以用細明體或其他中文字型的 abc。為甚麼？因為間隔不對。如果習慣讀英文，看這種間隔，讀不下去。如果用中文字型寫 abc 送到國外，國外電腦讀不出中文系統，很可能全篇變亂碼。所以勸大家，每次寫 abc，哪怕是幾個字母，養成習慣變成英文字型。

Never use Chinese fonts to write English letters!

Chapter 08 完成式：時間軸持續的表現法

❖ 現在完成式：

基本型態：S have PP

現在完成式表示事情過去開始，延續到現在，還沒有結束，還能再發展。例如，He was here for two hours，他曾經在這裏兩個小時，但離開了，現在不在這兒；至于發生在何時，不知道。He has been here for two hours，他兩個小時前來，現在還在此，尚未離開。

Did you go to a Mets game this season? 與 Have you gone to a Mets game this season? 差在哪？
Did you go? 表示球季已經結束了，現在沒機會看。
Have you gone? 球季還沒結束，還有機會看。

如果時間範圍已經結束，不可以用現在完成式。不可以說 Have you talked to him last month? 錯誤示範！

❖ 現在完成進行式

基本型態：S have been Ving

強調事情從過去開始，現在仍然發生。口語常用進行式；在口頭上，現在完成進行式往往與現在完成式通用。

比較：It has rained for an hour today.
或許斷續下雨，從早上累積一小時。
It has been raining for an hour.
一小時前開始下，現在還在下，未間斷。

❖ 過去完成式

基本型態：S had PP

過去完成式，通常表示時間順序：過去完成式發生在過去式之前。

比較：It rained when I hung out the clothes to dry.
我掛衣服時下雨：平行。
It had rained when I hung out the clothes to dry.
我掛衣服之前，下過雨：前後。

比較：We had decided to cancel the hike when we heard thunder.
已經決定取消登山活動，而後聽到雷聲。
We decided to cancel the hike when we heard thunder.
有因果：因為聽到雷聲，決定取消登山活動。

敍述故事，過去完成式代表過去式，不可或缺。

She saw the deer that they had heard last night. It had walked up so quietly that she didn't notice it until it was right by the garage.

> Ever 比較少用在肯定句。
>
> He has ever been there.（錯誤示範！）💣，現在完成式表示「曾經」，不需加 ever。

❖ 過去完成進行式

基本型態：**S had been Ving**

作用類似現在完成進行式，但是過去的事情，有前後。

He had been singing for forty minutes when she finally asked him to stop. 歌聲沒有間斷。

❖ 未來完成式

基本型態：**S will have PP**

比較少用，但還須具備。表示到未來某一個時間點，將要發生多久。

By this fall, we'll have known each other for fifteen years：我們現在認識了十四年又七個月，湊個整數，算到秋天剛好十五年。

❖ 未來完成進行式

基本型態：**S will have been Ving**

作用類似現在完成進行式，但指的是未來的事情。

She started swimming 58 minutes ago. In another 2 minutes, she will have been swimming for an hour.

過去完成、未來完成，表示時間的前後，所以很少連續很多句用此二態。

Combine these words into sentences.

注意完成式的用法。

1. Jacob / sleeping / ten o'clock / last night
2. Emily / written / ten pages / report / Anatomy / Tuesday
3. she / not / seen / exhibit / plans / visit / gallery / tomorrow / she / time
4. by / time / he / remembers / water / plants / will / wilted
5. when / passengers / allowed / board / plane / will / waiting / lounge / six hours

參考例句

1. **Jacob has been sleeping since ten o'clock last night.**
   Jacob went to sleep at ten o'clock last night.
   Jacob has been asleep since ten o'clock last night.

2. **Emily has written ten pages of her report for Anatomy since Tuesday.**
   Emily has written ten pages of her Anatomy report since Tuesday.
   Since Tuesday, Emily has written ten pages of her Anatomy report.
   Emily had written ten pages of her report for Anatomy by Tuesday.

評：還有一種可能：Emily has written ten pages of her Anatomy report for Tuesday.（未來的）星期二要交的報告，已經寫了十頁，還需再寫。過去完成式的句子，表示在過去的星期二之前，她已經寫過十頁。

❸ **She has not seen the exhibit, so she plans to visit the gallery tomorrow when she has time.**

評：She did not see the exhibit，展覽已經結束了，現在沒機會看了。
She has not seen the exhibit，展覽尚未結束，還有機會看。

❹ **By the time he remembers to water the plants, they will have wilted.**
The plants will have wilted by the time he remembers to water them.

❺ **When the passengers are allowed to board the plane, they will have been waiting in the lounge for six hours.**
When the passengers are allowed to board the plane, they will have waited in the lounge for six hours.

評：亦可寫 they will have waited (been waiting) for six hours in the lounge，但通常地點先、時間後。

Combine these sentences.

1. Ashley plays tennis. She joined the tennis team last semester. It is the school team.
2. Samantha is working on her perspective drawing. She started working on it when she got up. She got up at six this morning. The drawing is for her Architectural Design course.
3. He came to Taiwan six years ago. He is still in Taiwan. Now he lives in Taichung. He moved there three years ago.
4. Kelly works in that company. The company is near the subway entrance. She began working in that company nineteen years ago. She still works there.
5. Sarah and Michael met each other when they were in high school. They got married nine years and eleven months ago. They are still married.

參考例句

1. **Ashley has been on the school tennis team since last semester.**
   Ashley has played on the school tennis team since last semester.

評：但寫，Ashley joined the school tennis team last semester，只知道成為隊員，但不知道後來參加的情況。把 join 想成「辦入會手續」，可能比較不會用錯。華人常出錯：She has joined the team since last semester. 💣，辦完入會手續就結束了，用過去式，不得用現在完成式。

❷ **Samantha has been working on her perspective drawing for her Architectural Design course since she got up at six this morning.**
Samantha has been working on her Architectural Design perspective drawing for her course since she got up at six this morning.

評：若要省 course 字，第一句要調整；第二句可以直接省，寫 Samantha has been working on her perspective drawing for Architectural Design 即可。
亦可寫 Samantha has been working on her perspective drawing for her Architectural Design course since getting up at six this morning，但稍嫌不順。

❸ **He has been in Taiwan for six years, and has lived in Taichung for three years.**

評：假設寫 He has been in Taiwan for six years, and lived in Taichung for three years，只知道在臺中住了三年、已經搬離了，但不知何時。

❹ **Kelly has worked in that company near the subway entrance for nineteen years.**

❺ **Sarah and Michael have known each other since high school, and next month, they will have been married for ten years.**

Improve these sentences.

❶ There team which is comprised of four staffs have work yesterday for six hour concerning this future upcoming event whereupon General Manager shall except Service Award from Mayor.

❷ He have study Chemistry on university, is his major, while he did related work for three year after retired from military service in army.

❸ Many place around world grow coffee and most of these place around the world the coffee they growing the name "Robusta" kind of coffee and they grow "Robusta" because "Arabica" is easy to have disease but "Robusta" not easy to get disease but "Robusta" is having more caffeine than Arabica had it is by two time and one half mor cafeen.

❹ The discussion, manager versus directors, has been starting for two hours before lunch concerning the future plan for next season following this one and then they can't keep going due to the fact that suddenly there is no electricity

❺ Price fall, so farmer need to have more land so they borrow from bank but to farm more land they were reliant on expensive farm machinery, which they had to buy at very, very high price and cost much money to keep in good working order, and these bad things keep making things more bad and they can't get away.

參考例句

❶ **Their team, composed of four people, worked for six hours yesterday on the upcoming event in which the General Manager will accept a Service Award from the Mayor.**

評：There，那裏；their，他們的；they're，they are。Comprise，包含；compose，組成。可以寫 the team comprises four people，亦可寫 the team is composed of four people。寫 their four person team，或許每隊人數不同。Staff 是集合名詞，單位所有人員總共加起來的集合名詞。公司只有一個 staff。複數 staffs 指若干杖、棍。Yesterday 已經結束了，所以不適用現在完成式。Hours：注意單、複數。又 future 又 upcoming，重複，刪一。Whereupon、shall，古字，少用為妙。General Manager、Mayor 是職銜，不是名字，所以須加冠詞。句子略嫌長。

寫作撇步：一句一口氣。

❷ **He majored in Chemistry in college, and did related work for three years after his discharge from the army. His college major was Chemistry, and after his discharge from army, he did related work for three years.**

評：大學已經畢業，所以不符現在完成式的條件：改過去式。
Years：注意單、複數。
While 可以當「而」，但無論如何，猶有「同時」的含義。讀大學與退伍後三年怎麼可能「同時」？職業軍人當兵幾十年退伍，才可用 retired。一般服兵役、當十年兵退伍，叫做 be discharged。Discharge 動詞名詞兼用。

College or university?
一般口頭將「大學」說 college，除非講學校名稱。
例：She's a college student; she goes to Lesley University.

❸ **Most of the coffee grown worldwide is Robusta because it is more disease resistant than Arabica, even though it has two and a half times as much caffeine as Arabica.**
Even though it has 2.5 times more caffeine than Arabica, Robusta is more disease resistant, so most of the coffee grown worldwide is Robusta.
Globally, Robusta is more commonly grown than Arabica because although it has two and a half times more caffeine, it is more disease resistant than Arabica.

評：太多引號，版面凌亂。英文引號有規矩（請參 Chapter 11）；妄加引號，表示反諷。大寫即可。
注意時態、動詞型態、單複數、拼音。

❹ **In the morning, the discussion between the manager and directors concerning plans for the next season had continued for two hours before being interrupted by a power blackout.**

評：Versus 表示敵對、勝負必決的衝突，不等于 and。
Before lunch，語義模糊，只能當作 morning。

注意：過去式與現在完成式的性質；start 是轉捩點，一開始，接下去的事情就發生，所以不適合用現在完成式。

Plan 勢必是未來的，不加 future。
Next season 當然是 following this one，不必贅述。
Due to the fact that 一語沒有存在的必要：because 足矣。
記得標點。

❺ **Falling prices had forced farmers to borrow money from banks to buy more land to farm, which made them rely on expensive machinery, trapping them in a vicious cycle.**

評：注意單、複數。形容詞不如名詞，名詞不如動詞：be reliant on，形容詞，三字；rely on，動詞，二字。理所當然，機械需要保養；除非需要強調 maintenance，不必贅述，以免焦點散開。

Practice Writing

Complete these sentences. Don't be boring.

As the fog rolled in over the coast, ______________

Alfred washed his hands for the fifteenth time that hour, all the time telling himself ________________________

Sarah waited eagerly for the sound of the boss' car, because ________________

The hand grenade flew __________________

He felt the cat had been watching him all evening, and ____________ ____________

Write a sentence for each of these words.

- sturdy
- indebted
- shovel
- dissent
- haunted

Write an essay

Write about your hobby or some interest you have. Describe how you became interested in this, what benefits it brings you, and mention any disadvantages it may have. Give details, tell a story.

▶▶

Chapter 09 助動詞：輔助動詞意義的表達

動詞，如 **should, will, may, might, must, had better** 等。

基本句型：

現在式：助動詞 ＋ 原型動詞

過去式：助動詞 ＋ **have + PP**

這不是文法課本，所以本章只提幾個助動詞。最容易講解的是 should：

He should go. Should he go? He should not go. 現在式：應該。

He should have gone. Should he have gone? He should not have gone. **Should** 的過去式帶否定的意思：應該，但沒有。

must 在現代用法，通常是推測的結論、判斷：在室內工作，看到進來的人都帶濕傘，判斷：It must be raining。並不是命令要下雨。文字上，must 仍保留「必須」的用法。

本書不涵蓋古英文：本猩字彙沒有 shall 此字。may 與 might 都是現在式，過去式是 may have PP 、might have PP。

Combine these words into sentences.

❶ we / should / always / fasten / seatbelt / car

❷ Chloe / might / need / apply / new / passport / before long / old / expires / end / this year

❸ Tiffany / must / speak / Swahili / ophthalmologist / East Africa / fifteen years

❹ Kyle / must / forgotten / wallet / it / still / sitting / counter

❺ Amanda / had better / doctor / might / hurt / head / when / fell

參考例句

❶ **You should always fasten your seatbelt when you are in a car.**
You should always fasten your seatbelt in a car.

評：若寫 You should always fasten your seatbelt when you are in the car，似乎只坐我們這台車才需要繫安全帶。

> 英文句子必定要主詞；若泛指所有人，正確的主詞是 you。One 屬十九世紀英文，用在句子很難順；加上，現代人很不習慣。We 限定範圍，不涵所有人；但所有人上車需繫安全帶，所以用 you 爲妥。

❷ **Chloe might need to apply for a new passport before long, because her old one expires at the end of this year.**

❸ **Tiffany must speak Swahili since she was an ophthalmologist in East Africa for fifteen years.**
Tiffany must speak Swahili because she worked as an ophthalmologist in East Africa for fifteen years.

評：亦可寫 Tiffany must speak Swahili since she worked with an ophthalmologist in East Africa for fifteen years，她陪伴眼科醫師。

❹ **Kyle must have forgotten his wallet, because it is still sitting on the counter.**

❺ **Amanda had better see a doctor, because she might have hurt her head when she fell.**

Combine into one sentence.

1. We were in the library. Maybe it rained at that time.
2. The car is very, very dirty. It was up to Anthony to wash it. He didn't wash it. He played a video game all afternoon. The name of the video game is Dragons and Dungeons. The car is still very, very dirty.
3. He trained people in a very, very unusual way. It was not the same method as other people used. However, we think that his method was good. That is because the people who worked for him learned quickly. After the training course, they did their work efficiently.
4. Madison will finish the presentation this morning. Her presentation is about archeology. Archeologists excavated in India. They found remnants of sesame that had been cooked and lightly burned. This means that the sesame was farmed by people and did not grow wild, which means that farmers were growing sesame that long ago. That must have happened 5500 years ago. This is as far back as the record goes for farmers growing sesame. Before that, nobody grew this crop.
5. Jocelyn has to go to work in the morning. Making up her face takes a lot of time. She does not always have that much time. A lot of the time, Jocelyn uses a concealer under her eyes. If she does not do that, she looks like a panda. That may be all she uses.

參考例句

1. It may have rained while we were in the library.
2. Anthony should have washed the car, but he spent the afternoon playing Dragons and Dungeons instead, so the car is still filthy.
3. His unorthodox training method must have worked, because his staff learned quickly and worked efficiently.
4. This morning, Madison will finish her presentation about archeological excavations in India, where charred remnants of sesame dating back 5500 years indicate the earliest domestication of sesame.
5. Since she does not have time to do a full face of makeup every morning before going to work, Jocelyn frequently uses only a concealer under her eyes so she does not look like a panda.

Improve these sentences.

1. Hopefully, your presentation will be successful in terms of persuading boss invest this here project of yours that you propose to her.

2. Van Gogh had close friends in Arles, one of the closest, and a favorite sitter there was the local postman, his name was Joseph Roulin, and Roulin cared in 1888 for the artist because happened severe onset mental illness, the following year then Roulin saw him into the hospital, and Roulin assisted van Gogh as he (van Gogh) recuperated and returned to normal life.

3. During the period of time of the coronavirus crisis which occurred in the year 2020, the Parliament of Hungary granted the power to rule by decree without any time limit to Prime Minister Viktor Orbán, who is a Far-Right Politician, despite the fact that Opposition Parties engaged in efforts to set a time limit.

4. The "Ever Given" is the name of a ship. The ship is leased by the Evergreen group. It is four hundred meters long. It was going through the Suez Canal. On March 23, 2021, strong winds blew. They struck the ship very hard. The winds blew against the ship so hard that the ship got stuck on the shore of the Canal and could not be moved. No other ships could go through the Canal because of this. The situation continued for a week. Finally, after a week, workers made the ship float again. They freed it from the shore.

5. Lapis lazuli is a semi-precious stone that comes from Afghanistan and the Indus Valley, and it was used during the Renaissance period to produce a color called indigo and of all the pigments they are, indigo is the most expensive in price.

參考例句

❶ **I hope your presentation succeeds in persuading the boss to invest in the project you propose.**
I hope your presentation persuades the boss to invest in your proposed project.

❷ **One of van Gogh's closest friends and favorite sitters in Arles was the local postman, Joseph Roulin, who cared for the artist during a severe onset of mental illness in 1888, saw him into the hospital the following year, and assisted him as he recuperated and returned to normal life.**

❸ **During the 2020 coronavirus crisis, Hungary's Parliament granted far-right Prime Minister Viktor Orbán the power to rule by decree indefinitely, even though opposition parties tried to set a time limit on those powers.**

評：再強調：盡量不要寫 the fact that。

❹ **The Evergreen group's 400 meter long container ship, the Ever Given, was buffeted by strong winds in the Suez Canal on March 23, 2021, wedging it into the shore and blocking the Canal for a week before it could be floated free.**

評：船名已大寫，無需引號。船名亦可斜體。
多背常用單字。

❺ **Lapis lazuli, a semi-precious stone from Afghanistan and the Indus Valley, was used during the Renaissance to produce indigo, the most expensive of all pigments.**

Practice Writing

Complete these sentences. Don't be trite or vague.

On my flight across the Pacific, the man in the next seat __________

In the pawnshop __________

The clock over the door ____________________

A large antelope wandered ____________________

Two hundred small glass beads on her dress ____________________

Write a sentence for each of these words.

- dispose
- recuperate
- declare
- explode
- split

Write an essay.

Write about a food you really dislike. What's wrong with it? Why don't you like it? What does it taste like?

Chapter 10 被動：凸顯受詞的地位

基本型態：**Object be PP**
Object be PP by S

被動強調受詞；也許主詞不重要。
被動語氣，不宜太常用，但有其必要，也有其妙用。
Elvis was seen in a restaurant.
貓王被看見；誰看到他，不是重點。不知主詞是誰，也用被動。

The doctor had a feeling that she was being watched as she made her rounds.

Sheep were probably domesticated about 10,000 BCE, in Mesopotamia.

A majority is required to pass the bill.

Women have not been treated as equals.

重點是主詞不用被動：
Amber saw Taylor Swift in concert last weekend.
不要寫 Taylor Swift was seen in concert last weekend by Amber. 💣

若從上下文很容易判斷主詞，可以用被動。例如，文章討論印度政府推行教育，寫：In rural India, not every village is provided with a school. 因為已經明白推行教育的是政府，所以不必寫。

官僚、公司常用被動來逃避責任。The Administration admitted that mistakes had been made. 💣 或 The oil company said that oil had been spilled in the nature preserve. 💣

學生用被動掩飾研究的疏略。The chemical element bismuth was officially discovered in the 18th century 💣（可是我懶得查出是誰發現的）。

不要太多被動。尤其理工報告，幾乎找不到主詞。因為學者 — 尤其理工 — 濫用被動，所以很多寫作老師嚴禁被動，但確實有它的好處。很多直述句串在一起，偶來個被動，效果不錯。

These sentences should be turned into the passive.

不必要的主詞可省。

1. Somebody locks the door to the storeroom every evening.
2. The police detonated the abandoned suitcase, in case it was a bomb.
3. People leave many umbrellas on the Taipei MRT every day.
4. Following the 1988 coffee crisis, when supply outbalance demand, they introduced trade fair certification.
5. A powerful earthquake hit central Taiwan early on September 21, 1999, and destroyed the Wenwu Temple.

參考例句

❶ **The door to the storeroom is locked every evening.**

❷ **The police detonated the abandoned suitcase, in case it was a bomb.**
The abandoned suitcase was detonated, in case it was a bomb.

評：又 suitcase 又 in case，不漂亮。可改為 The abandoned suitcase was detonated lest it was a bomb. The abandoned suitcase was detonated for fear that it was a bomb. The abandoned suitcase was detonated out of fear that it was a bomb.

❸ **Many umbrellas are left on the Taipei MRT every day.**

評：讀者未必懂 MRT。若有疑慮，寫出來：Mass Rapid Transit. 不必說明是 people 遺失的，除非你看過鴨嘴獸把傘留在捷運上。

❹ **Following the 1988 coffee crisis, when supply outbalanced demand, fair trade certification was introduced.**

❺ **Central Taiwan was hit by a powerful earthquake early on September 21, 1999, destroying the Wenwu Temple.**
The Wenwu Temple was destroyed by a powerful earthquake which hit central Taiwan early on September 21, 1999.

評：各句重點不同。

These sentences are to be improved.

1. To seal the envelope, pressure should be applied.
2. Most others regions are lagged far behind by Taiwan in terms of the production of renewable energy.
3. The self-portrait "Yo Picasso" was painted by Pablo Picasso in 1901 at the age of 19.
4. The building was fallen off of by me while the roof was being fixed by me and that experience will never be forgotten by myself.
5. Breakfast would have been served by Ashley, but the oven broke and nobody could fix it before ten.

參考例句

1. **Press to seal the envelope.**

2. **Taiwan lags far behind most other regions in producing renewable energy.**
   In producing renewable energy, Taiwan lags far behind most other regions.

評：第一句尚可，但因為 regions，讀者很自然認為介系詞片語說明地點，如 regions in Asia；因此，介系詞片語移句首。更好的方法，換寫法：Taiwan produces far less renewable energy than most other regions.

❸ **Pablo Picasso painted the self-portrait, Yo Picasso, in 1901 at the age of 19.**
At the age of 19, Pablo Picasso painted the self-portrait, Yo Picasso (1901).

評：選主動、被動，依重點而決定。

畫名大寫即可，不加引號。可斜體。

❹ **I will never forget falling off the building while I was fixing the roof.**
I will never forget falling off the building while fixing the roof.

評：forget to V，忘記要做某件事；forget Ving，忘記做過某件事。

❺ **Ashley would have served breakfast, but there was something wrong with the oven, and it could not be fixed before ten.**

評：The oven broke，表示烤箱破掉了、裂了，很難想像；似乎是故障，但因為細節不明，所以簡單寫 something was wrong with the oven。亦可寫 the oven was not working properly；若非正式文章，可寫 the oven was on the blink。

Practice Writing

Complete these sentences. Can you develop each one into a story?

The Prince told his father ____________________

We cried during the movie because ____________________

At the movie, we laughed when ____________________

As we watched the movie, our popcorn ____________________

Everybody got up to dance ______________________________________

Write a sentence for each of these words.

- remorseless
- penetrate
- confine
- sprout
- thaw

Write an essay

Describe a typhoon to someone who has never been in one. What should you do during a typhoon? What should you not do?

Chapter 11 標點符號：讓字句自帶節奏

標點符號很重要，很多人寫中文，不太注意標點，只會逗點，連句點都沒有，一路逗點到底，還、有、一、種、人、每、一、字、加、頓、號、不、相、信、的、話、去、問、高、中、國、文、老、師、這樣寫的人卻不了解，標點符號作用很大，讀者或知中華古書原無句讀閱者讀誦斷句必明瞭文意方知批圈古人僅讀與句未知問號讀者頓也句者斷句也其後西潮東來文人知標點妙用，運用恰當，可以增強字句的節奏，文意因以暢明，讀者比較容易看懂，不需要回頭整理句子。

Periods 句點

句子語意完整，不是問句，寫句點。

This is a complete sentence.
We are not finished yet.

縮寫。全句末字縮寫，一個句點就好了。但盡量避免這種寫法。

Dr. Jimenez was born on Nov. 12, 1981, in St. Louis, MO., U.S.A..
Dr. Jimenez was born on Nov. 12, 1981, in St. Louis, MO., U.S.A.

行文的月份、州名不該縮寫。

Dr. Jimenez was born on November 12, 1981, in St. Louis, Missouri, U.S.A.

人名簡寫，**initials**，嚴格說應該加句點，但往往省略。

John Fitzgerald Kennedy 總統的 initials 為 J.F.K.，又如 Dr. Martin Luther King, Jr. 縮寫 M.L.K. 但通常寫 JFK、MLK。

一行首位，不可寫句點。

句點前不可以留空格，句點後必須留一空格。

They paid their debt . Only later did they discover that something was wrong. 💣

They paid their debt.Only later did they discover that something was wrong. 💣

句點後空兩格現在視為錯誤；句點後只要空一格。

句點置引號裏面。

He's not sure how to pronounce "quinoa". 💣

He's not sure how to pronounce "quinoa."

The teacher said, "If nobody has any questions, we'll have a test". 💣

The teacher said, "If nobody has any questions, we'll have a test."

若括弧附註次要內容，句點置括弧外；若整句在括弧內，句點置括弧內。

They paid NT$3,000 for the seats (about US$100.) 💣

They paid NT$3,000 for the seats (about US$100).

> Keep your page clean. 句點太多，版面凌亂，所以現在省略很多縮寫的句點：USA, LA, CE, BCE。
>
> 醫師、先生，美國仍保留句點：Dr., Mr.；本猩喜歡英國用法，省略：Dr Jimenez, Mr Petrović.

Commas 逗點

中文叫做「逗點」或「逗號」；停留、停頓的意思。句未完，須分隔內容、換氣。日期也用。

Caroline talked to Brandon and Vanessa phoned Colin.
讀者很自然以為 Caroline 跟 Brandon 與 Vanessa 講話，看到 phoned 才知道是兩回事，Caroline 與 Brandon 講話，之外，Vanessa 打電話給 Colin。不要增加讀者的負擔；語意要清楚，加逗點。

Caroline talked to Brandon, and Vanessa phoned Colin. 一目瞭然。

加逗點，句意明瞭。逗點也會改變句意。
Thank you for helping Brian. 謝謝你幫助 Brian。
Thank you for helping, Brian. 謝謝 Brian 的幫忙。
Be honest if you can't be kind. 若不能厚道，該誠實。
Be honest. If you can't, be kind. 要誠實；若不能，要厚道。

多個形容詞形容一名詞，用逗點隔開。若不知道該不該加逗點，加 **and**：如果適合，就用逗點。

Andrew fretted through the long, sleepless night，可以寫成 Andrew fretted through the long and sleepless night，所以此處加逗點無誤。

逗點，comma，兩個 m。一個 m 的 coma，昏迷不醒。

Jacob enjoys traditional Chinese paintings. 不可加，因為不可改 Jacob enjoys traditional and Chinese paintings；traditional 修飾 Chinese paintings： Chinese paintings 是一個單元，所以不加逗點。

還有一個測試的方法，把形容詞調位；如果還通，就加逗點；形容詞雖然有一定的順序，但可以調位測試。

Avery is a cheerful, slim, lively seven year old. 換成
Avery is a slim, lively, cheerful seven year old. 或
Avery is a slim, cheerful, lively seven year old.
可。但不要堆砌太多形容詞，不然寫成 Avery is a short, slim, lively, cheerful, humorous, mischievous, active, curious seven year old 💣，不像文章，像字彙練習。
Avery is a happy little girl. 不必加逗點。加逗點，讓語意明瞭，不費工也不貴，所以如果可能有疑問，還是加。

如果列二項，不加逗點：
The photographer photographed Christian and Lionel.

列出三個項目，第二項目後加逗點。這是所謂的 **Oxford comma**，亦名 serial comma.
The photographer photographed Christian, Lionel, and Milica.

如果不加 Oxford comma，或許語意不同或不清楚。
寫 The photographer photographed the football players, Christian and Lionel，到底拍了幾個人？或許拍了 football players 之外又拍了 Christian 與 Lionel。如果施用 Oxford comma，意義容易區別。

The photographer photographed the football players, Christian and Lionel. 拍了兩位球員的照片，名字是 Christian、Lionel。

The photographer photographed the football players, Christian, and Lionel. 至少四人的照片：球員（兩個以上）、Christian、Lionel。

需要 Oxford comma？有那麼重要嗎？

參考：美國五十州，有四十三州的法律規定官方文章必須按照規則用 Oxford comma；國會上下院也如此規定。

逗點不可居一行首位。可居列行末位。逗點前不可以留空格，逗點後必須留一空格。

Ben was not sure where to put the comma ,so he guessed.

Ben was not sure where to put the comma, so he guessed.

寫對話，引號前加逗點。

Nathan said, “I have to get to work now.”

“I have to go to work now,” Nathan said.

I spent all morning putting in a comma and all afternoon taking it out.

愛爾蘭詩人、劇作家／Oscar Wilde

Question marks 問號

問號比較簡單：用來表示問句。Is that right?
問號不可居一行首位。可居列行末位。問號前不可以留空格，問號後必須一留空格。問號通常在引號內。
Alyssa asked, “Did you see that?”

但若引用他人肯定句，在引號外。
Do you know who said, “The pen is mightier than the sword”?

Exclamation marks 驚嘆號

驚嘆號！亦名 exclamation point ！要省著用！驚嘆號，表示驚訝、興奮、命令、意外、感嘆。但最好還是用內容表示驚訝等，不要依賴標點達到驚嘆的效果。

驚嘆號不可居一行首位。可居列行末位。驚嘆號前不可以留空格，驚嘆號後必須留一空格。驚嘆號通常在引號內。
Morgan flung the door open and shouted, “Chloe just rammed your car into the river!”

如果不確定要不要加驚嘆號，不加。頂多一個驚嘆號；要發表的文章，兩個驚嘆號以上，不適合。簡訊則無妨。

Quotation marks 引號

引用字句，用引號。對話，用引號。引全句，首字母大寫；引片語，不大寫。一句分開，後段加引號。

The teacher said, “Study hard.”

We soon understood why the reviews said the movie was “pretentious, boring, and poorly directed.”

“You may write on any topic you please,” the teacher said, “just so long as you turn in your assignment on time.”

如果所說的話不止一段，段尾不收引號，下文每段以引號起，到話講完，收引號。

如果沒有斜體字，書名、文章名可以用引號。

“The Innocents Abroad” is not Mark Twain’s best work, but it is a lot of fun.

單大寫，亦可。

The Innocents Abroad is not Mark Twain’s best work, but it is a lot of fun.

最好用斜體字：

The Innocents Abroad is not Mark Twain’s best work, but it is a lot of fun.

介紹專用術語，可以用引號（雙引號；不可用單引號）：

A single strap knotted onto the legs of a falcon or other hunting raptor is called a “jess.”

> 不正式用法，quotation marks 可說 quotes。

要求讀者解讀字意，可以用引號；往往表示反諷、戳破假象、故意講反話。英語系國家的人本來就喜歡 sarcasm 講反話。口語依語調表示，但書寫沒有語調，用引號吧：She “loved” the gift. 一點都不喜歡禮物。

句點、逗點在引號內。

不正式信件的稱謂後加逗點：
Dear Halus,
假若文章首句引某一句，為了排版美觀，往往省除第一括弧。
雙引號還有特殊用法，表示英吋：10” 即十英吋，但這種寫法，限草稿、圖表用。完稿時要修正成 ten inches。

以上論雙引號。引號中須加引號，用單引號：
I asked why Sean was smiling. He said, “I just read a funny quote by A A Milne, the man who wrote Winnie the Pooh. He said, ‘People say nothing is impossible, but I do nothing every day.’”

雙引號通常引講出的話；單引號引內心獨白。
“Yes, of course, sir, the customer is always right,” Alyssa concurred with a forced smile, thinking, ‘Pompous idiot.’

中文沒有大小寫，斜體很少用，所以往往加強語氣用「引號」。看過學生幫老師寫推薦函，寫He is a “good” student，以爲是加強語氣，適得其反；美國教授看，以爲老師打暗號，暗示這個學生爛透，可是不方便明講（或許怕學生報復）。

這種情形要加強語氣怎麼辦呢？多背單字吧！ He is an excellent student, a superb student，均可，但猶嫌空洞：如何個好法？

Colons 冒號

冒號等于「換句話說」、「我的意思是」。冒號後不大寫，除非專用名字。
You know how to improve your English: practice.
All contestants will be required to bring: their bow, arrows, a quiver, and any shooting gloves or arm protectors.
The investigation revealed the culprit: Donald Turnip.

正式信件的稱謂後加冒號：
Dear Admissions Committee:

冒號不可居一行首位。可居列行末位。冒號前不可以留空格，冒號後必須留一空格。

Semicolons 分號

分號即逗點上加句點，表示停頓：長於逗點，短於句點。強調兩句關聯，要縮短距離，用分號：
There was a lunar eclipse last night; we were not surprised it rained.

Email 的性質簡短扼要，因而容易語氣衝，用分號可以緩和。
The report from the Accounting office came. There's nothing we can do. We need more assistance.
分三句，有埋怨語氣，讀者可能不悅。用分號，看的人比較舒服。
The report from the accounting office came; there's nothing we can do. We need more assistance.

分號可界定意義。

The tennis player served eggs were thrown onto the court. 乍看以為 the tennis player served eggs. 球員端上了雞蛋。看到 were thrown 才知道不對，讀者緊急煞車。

The tennis player served; eggs were thrown onto the court. 其實，可以分兩句，但這樣寫的好處是因果清楚、緊湊。

需要分號卻下逗點，名為 comma splice，很容易處理：逗點改分號。

The team kept fumbling the ball, they lost the game.

The team kept fumbling the ball; they lost the game.

太多逗點，眼花，某些狀況可以用分號。

Before moving to Colorado, they had lived in Benzonia, Michigan, Waynoka, Oklahoma, and Medicine Bow, Wyoming.

改用分號就清楚。

Before moving to Colorado, they had lived in Benzonia, Michigan; Waynoka, Oklahoma; and Medicine Bow, Wyoming.

分號可以讓文章比較順暢、多變化。

Namely, however, therefore 前往往加分號。

It seemed there was only one man who could stop the Confederates; namely, Ulysses S Grant.

'However' is rarely used in common speech; however, it may be used in formal speech and in writing.

Apostrophes 撇號

撇號主要注明所有格、擁有：

We saw Juan’s car in the parking lot.
Mitch McConnell’s name will go down in infamy.

區別單、複數所有格：

the bus driver’s route 一位公車司機的路線
the bus drivers’ route 多位公車司機的路線
the Smiths’ house 即 Smith 他們一家人的房子。

Drivers、Smiths 是複數名詞，最後字母是 s，所以撇號後可不加 s，因為講話時不發音。想加就請便。單數名詞，如 Charles 的所有格發 s 音，Charles’s 亦可寫 Charles’；rhinoceros 的所有格， rhinoceros’s 亦可寫 rhinoceros’，而 s 結尾的單數名詞，還是建議撇號後加 s。

撇號又名省字號、縮寫號，因爲可以將兩三個字縮寫在一起：

That is not a good idea.
That’s not a good idea.
I would not have said that if I had known that you did not know.
I wouldn’t’ve said that if I’d known you didn’t know.

除非寫不正式文章、對話，一般寫作不縮寫。
省略數字，可用撇號：要注意，因為一般臺灣的用法不合英文的規則。1971 年可以寫成 ’71，但如果寫 71’，意思為七十一英尺。

特殊情形，撇號可以代表複數。
Cross your T's and dot your I's.
The great composer Telemann composed most of his work in the 1700's.

本猩的看法，為了版面清爽，可以省這幾個撇號，直寫 Ts、Is、1700s. 但如果句子可能讓讀者將 Is 看成 is，還是加撇號。用法要一致。
除非特殊情形，若把's 當複數，是純種不學無術的特級笨蛋。
有的撇號很重要。不想被看成笨蛋，it's、its 必須分清楚。It's 等于 it is 或完成式的 it has 的縮寫（現在式無此寫法）。Its 是 it 的所有格。
Whose 是所有格，誰的？ Who's 是 who is 或完成式的 who has 的縮寫。

Hyphens and dashes 連字號、破折號

Hyphen 連字號與 dash 破折號，一連一破。
字太長，行列寫不完，用 hyphen 連到下一行。分字有規矩，不在本書範圍內。唯一要提的是，分字最好在中間：例如，分 unquestionably 最好分 unques-tionably，若分 un-questionably 💣、unquestion-ably 💣 或 unquestionab-ly 💣，失衡，看不舒服、讀者分心。

In her most recent paper, Professor Piggs discussed the inter-dependence of symbiotic relationships.
Hyphen 把相關的字連上，例如 up-to-date、sister-in-law。
數字寫出來，可用 hyphen 分：We saw thirty-one deer.
寫分數，用連字號：three-fourths.
有的頭銜可加連字號：vice-president

Hyphen 前後不加空格。若斷字，可置行末，但不得置行首。

> 英文往往把兩個字用連字號連，久了變成一個字，如 fire fly 變 fire-fly，現在寫 firefly。

Dash — 破折號 – 前後空格。破折號表示停頓，可以代替其它如括弧、逗點等標點增添變化。

They delivered the books (all 300 of them) two weeks late.

They delivered the books – all 300 of them – two weeks late.

若標點不清楚，破折號可以讓讀者容易了解。

Essential items, his spare gloves, his extra hat, and his flashlight, were in the backpack which slid down the glacier.

Essential items – his spare gloves, his extra hat, his flashlight – were in the backpack which slid down the glacier.

寫對話，破折號表示說話停頓。

Don sputtered, “But, but – how could – you expect me to know?”

非正式文章中代替冒號，強調結果。

The judge announced the victory for: Michael.

The judge announced the victory for – Michael.

Her dog chewed up my shoes and she expected me to like him.

Her dog chewed up my shoes and she expected me to – like him.

隱藏字，可以破折號表示。

M--- wished to remain anonymous.

Just before he got shot, the suspect shouted out, “F--- the police!”

表示範圍。

You will be tested on pages 17 – 240.

In 497 – 509CE, the Hephthalites (known in Chinese as the 嚈噠 Yeda), pushed from Turfan north to Ürümqi.

數字用破折號。

By the bottom of the fifth inning, the score was 3 – 0.

破折號也可以表示連接。

All seats on the Podgorica – Belgrade flight were sold out.

除非妳是美國詩人 Emily Dickinson，不要太多破折號。

波浪號 ～ tilde 在英文很少用。草稿可以表示「大約」：~ 20。

完稿，寫出 approximately 20 或 approximately twenty.

為甚麼 hyphens 重要？請比較：

twenty five-year-old horses

廿匹五歲的馬

twenty-five year-old horses

廿五匹一歲的馬

twenty-five-year-old horses

廿五歲的馬

打 Word 檔，空一格打兩個連字號再空一格，下個空格 Word 自動把兩個連字號連成破折號。

Ellipsis 省略號

省略號 ellipsis，顧名思義，省字。引用字句，不需要的字，用省略號。如果同一句中省略若干字，三點；若省句點，四點。五點，要下班。
原文：The Secretary is authorized in cases of emergency to incur such expenses as may be necessary (a) in searching for and rescuing, or in cooperating in the search for and rescue of, persons lost on the public lands.

引用：The Federal Land Policy and Management Act of 1976 (Sec. 312. [43 U.S.C. 1742]) states that "the Secretary is authorized to incur ... expenses... in searching for and rescuing ... persons lost on the public lands."

Helen Keller 原文：Security is mostly a superstition. It does not exist in nature, nor do the children of men as a whole experience it. Avoiding danger is no safer in the long run than outright exposure. Life is either a daring adventure, or nothing.

引用：Helen Keller said, "Security is mostly a superstition. It does not exist in nature.... Avoiding danger is no safer in the long run than outright exposure. Life is either a daring adventure, or nothing."

寫對話，表示話未講完：At the Battle of Spotsylvania Courthouse, General John Sedgwick was warned to hide from enemy snipers, to which he replied, "They couldn't hit an elephant at this dis..." 但除非寫意識流小說，盡量不要多用。該不該寫意識流小說，見仁見智。

Parentheses, brackets, and braces 括弧、方括弧、花括弧

Parentheses，括弧，亦稱 round brackets、圓括弧，( )。Brackets，方括弧，[ ]。Braces，花括弧又叫大括弧，{ }。

Parentheses 是複數名詞，單數 parenthesis。澄清、注明、題外話，用 **parentheses**。

Mark Twain (the pen name of Samuel Clemens) is one of America's finest authors.

Although blind, the British adventurer James Holman (1786 – 1857) traveled throughout Europe, Africa, Asia, Australia, and became the first blind person to circumnavigate the globe.

Irene started the day with a cup of coffee (as usual).

括弧常用來介紹縮寫。

You forgot to fill in the box for DOB (date of birth).

The Organization of Islamic Cooperation (OIC), founded in 1969, now has 57 member states.

括弧指示。

If you aren't familiar with the past perfect, there is a good place for you to practice (please see Chapter 8).

用括弧列項目。

To join the US Navy, you must (a) be an American citizen or permanent resident, (b) be from 17 to 34 years old, (c) have a high school education, (d) take the Vocational Aptitude test, and (e) pass a medical examination.

引用書、文。

When sharpening a drawknife, hold the drawknife steady and move the sharpening stone (Bealer, 1980).

左括弧前空格後不空格，右括弧前不空格後空格。左括弧可置行首，不可置行尾；右括弧不可置行首，可置行尾。句點、逗點等置右括弧外。但獨立句的句點在括弧內。

Finally, peace was made at Appomattox Courthouse. (This has been discussed in great detail by Bruce Catton.)

This should give you an idea of how to use parentheses. If you have a lot of material in parentheses (for example, if you need additional information [or even more information {and if that's not enough, even more information}]), you may nest them in brackets and braces. But avoid that, because it looks horrible.

Brackets 方括弧

原文沒有的字，引用時，以方括弧指出。第三者引文時用方括弧加內容澄清內容、代名詞。

原文：When the finance officer pressed the issue, she explained to him that a second mortgage was impossible under the existing circumstances.

The bank manager "explained to [the finance officer] that a second mortgage was impossible under the existing circumstances."

但這樣寫，版面不俐落，不如改寫：

The bank manager explained to the finance officer that "a second mortgage was impossible under the existing circumstances."

原文有誤，引用時用 sic（拉丁文，「如此」）說明；sic 可用斜體，方括弧不用斜體。
The Coahuiltecan were small, autonomous groups of Amerindians who inhibited [*sic*] the Rio Grande valley in what is now northeastern Mexico and southern Texas.
正確字眼是 inhabited，原文筆誤成 inhibited.

引用外語，英文翻譯寫在方括弧內。
It's just as the Serbs say, Бог је прво себи браду створио [God created the beard on himself first]; in other words, people always place their own interests first.

方括弧指出修改引用文大小寫。
"[T]here remain doubts about the veracity of his statements."
The paper reported "[s]imilar doubts remain concerning the evidence."

引用字句時加斜體字加強語氣，若原文無斜體，要說明。
"Approximately *sixteen million people* today can trace their lineage to Genghis Khan [emphasis added]."

刪除不雅字句，要說明。
He then allegedly drew his pistol and shouted, "I'm going to blow your [expletive] head off!"

Braces，花括弧，名稱很多，用途不大；主要用于程式、樂譜。雖然好看，但不當用來代替括弧或方括弧。

頓　號

頓號好用，但不知道看倌覺察到了嗎？頓號是中文的標點，英文沒有頓號。我看過不少臺灣學者寫英文論文還加頓號，卻沒有發覺字型不同、鍵盤不同。簡而言之，英文沒有頓號。

Correct the punctuation of these sentences.

1. The question has been raised however: whether the courts, including "the Supreme Court", which has sometimes been very unsympathetic to minority religions, such as the "Church of the Flying Spaghetti Monster," will allow discrimination to continue.

2. Mary Mallon, 1869 ~ 1938, was (an Irish) cook (in New York) who was an 'asymptomatic typhoid carrier', eventually causing perhaps as many as fifty fatalities because: she refused to wash her hands and earning the nickname: "Typhoid Mary."

3. With it's rich nutty ,flavor "sesame" sometimes also called "benne" is used, in cuisines around the world .

4. The length of the chip shortage boils down to one overarching factor a significant surge in demand; driven by digital transformation and accelerated by the pandemic. the accounting giant "*Deloitte*" asserted in a December 2021 analysis of the semiconductor shortage

5. As a teenager "NRA" National Rifle Association President, Harlon Carter, murdered (fifteen year old) Ramón Casiano because he, Casiano, was not afraid of the shotgun Carter was carrying.

參考例句

❶ **The question has been raised, however, whether the courts – including the Supreme Court, which has sometimes been very unsympathetic to minority religions such as the Church of the Flying Spaghetti Monster – will allow discrimination to continue.**

評：原句的逗點沒錯，但因為太多逗點，所以讀者容易眼花撩亂。此例逗點適合改破折號；括弧太重。

❷ **Mary Mallon (1869 – 1938) was an Irish cook in New York who was an asymptomatic typhoid carrier, eventually causing perhaps as many as fifty fatalities because she refused to wash her hands, and earning the nickname Typhoid Mary.**

❸ **With its rich, nutty, flavor, sesame, sometimes also called benne, is used in cuisines around the world.**

評：這句許多逗點難避免，若再加引號，版面不堪入目。
It’s、its 必分清楚。
逗點後需要空格。句點前不可空格。

❹ **"The length of the chip shortage boils down to one overarching factor: a significant surge in demand, driven by digital transformation and accelerated by the pandemic, "the accounting giant Deloitte asserted in a December 2021 analysis of the semiconductor shortage.**

評：逗點前不可加空格，後必加。句末需要句點。
公司名號大寫，不須引號，更不須斜體。

❺ **As a teenager, NRA (National Rifle Association) President Harlon Carter murdered fifteen-year-old Ramón Casiano because he (Casiano) was not afraid of the shotgun Carter was carrying.**

Punctuate these sentences.

1. She said come in and sit down

2. She said come in and sat down

3. Following his advisors advice Caleb planned to enroll in four courses Composition Geology Latin II and Introduction to Constitutional Law

> Latin II 即大二拉丁文、第二年拉丁文課程。

4. Arnold told Inspector Esposito Kenny told me Ted said A shipment of cocaine is arriving tomorrow night so I think you had better be prepared

5. Weve been lying around our homes embracing that pandemic induced 247 casual lifestyle sweatpants and sweatshirts but designers plan to lift us out of this comfortable rut with a new 2022 wardrobe blending nostalgic designs and enhanced basics

參考例句

1. **She said, "Come in and sit down."**

2. **She said, "Come in," and sat down.**

3. **Following his advisor's advice, Caleb planned to enroll in four courses: Composition, Geology, Latin II, and Introduction to Constitutional Law.**

4. **Arnold told Inspector Esposito, "Kenny told me Ted said, 'A shipment of cocaine is arriving tomorrow night,' so I think you had better be prepared."**
   Arnold told Inspector Esposito, "Kenny told me Ted said, 'A shipment of cocaine is arriving tomorrow night, so I think you had better be prepared.'"

評：若無標點，無法確定 I think you had better be prepared 是 Arnold 對 Inspector Esposito 說，或 Ted 對 Kenny 說。上列例句加了標點，第一句是 Arnold 對 Inspector Esposito 說，第二例句是 Ted 對 Kenny 說，了然分明。口說英語，語調不同，容易分辨，但書寫依賴標點。

5. **We've been lying around our homes, embracing that pandemic-induced 24/7 casual lifestyle – sweatpants and sweatshirts – but designers plan to lift us out of this comfortable rut, with a new 2022 wardrobe blending nostalgic designs and enhanced basics.**

這個逗點有點貴

百餘年前，美國一位富婆遊玩歐洲，看上了精緻手鐲，但是因為天價，決定打電報問先生，可以花七萬五千元美金買這只手鐲？（當時會計師年薪兩千美元、牙醫年薪兩千五百美元）。寫電報力求精簡，所以她寫了：

Saw beautiful bracelet. Price 75 thousand dollars. May I buy it?

丈夫回：No, price too high.

但打電報的人少打了一個逗點，所以太太看到的電報寫：
No price too high.

太太收到，樂不可支，飛奔去買。回國給先生看，先生暴跳如雷，問了究竟，告了電報公司，還告贏了。

Practice writing

Complete these sentences. Let your imagination fly.

The smell of the cooking ________

Just before the spaceship landed, ________

When he woke up that morning, he never expected ________

The pleasant sound of the water in the creek masked the sound of ________

Watching silently as the door slowly opened, they ________

Write a sentence for each of these words.

- thrilling
- tender
- flipped
- loot
- wagged

Write an essay.

If you had all the money and all the time you needed, where would you like to go for vacation? What would you do there? Why did you choose that place? Be specific, give details.

Chapter 12 大小寫：適用範圍與規矩

中文引英文字，往往每一字大寫：
他最近買了一支新的墨水筆（Fountain Pen）。💣

其實，英文大寫有一定的規則，這樣寫不對。應該寫 fountain pen 才對。簡單介紹大寫的規矩。最容易記得的規條是，不要全寫大寫，IT LOOKS LIKE YOU'RE SCREAMING AT THE READER AND IT'S VERY RUDE, SO DON'T DO THIS!

句子首字要大寫，專用名詞，如人名、地名、商標，要大寫。「我」，I，大寫。
When she was in Greece, Haley bought a bottle of Assyrtiko.
英文父子同名，父姓後加 Senior，通常縮寫 Sr.；兒姓後加 Junior，通常縮寫 Jr. 要大寫。Sr.、Jr. 前加不加逗點，看個人習慣。本猩不加，版面美觀。
Christopher Onions, Sr.
Christopher Onions Jr

頭銜大寫。
Ms O'Hara discussed Dr McCoy's data with Professor Grigoryan.

引用字句，首字大寫。
Frank Zappa said, "Jazz isn't dead. It just smells funny."

日、月、節日大寫，但季節不大寫。
Thanksgiving falls on the fourth Thursday of November.
My favorite season is winter.

國家、城市、族群大寫。

Sangpuy Katatepan Mavaliyw is a great Pinuyumayan singer from Katratripulr in southeastern Taiwan.

寫信收尾寫

Truly,
Wishing you all the best,

傳統的詩，每行首字大寫。現代詩，則不一定。

書、文章、電影、影集名有點複雜。首字、形容詞、名詞、動詞、尾字要大寫；簡而言之，冠詞、連接詞、介系詞不大寫，除非是首字。五個字母以上的字都大寫，所以書名若有 Between，雖是介系詞，大寫。末字要大寫。

The Elements of Style
The Catcher in the Rye
A Brief History of Time
The Secret of the Incas
The Phantom Tollbooth
The Path We Wandered Down

你看過幾部？
寫作要進步，
要多閱讀！

書名首字是冠詞，前面有所有格，要不要保留冠詞？有兩派。有人認為所有格加冠詞不合文法、不順，刪：Mark Twain's *Innocents Abroad*。有人認為書名是作者定的，不當改，保留：Mark Twain's *The Innocents Abroad*。均可。本猩偏向刪，因為句子讀起來比較順。

上文提及 O'Hara 與 McCoy；O'Hara 是愛爾蘭姓，McCoy 來自蘇格蘭，通常照此例大小寫，但各家或許有各家的習慣。

姓名大小寫也有區域色彩

講到姓名大小寫，頭就大。荷蘭姓的字首，若引全名，小寫。
Johannes van der Meer
N B ter Beek
Pieter van Hanrixma thoe Slooten
但只列姓不舉名，大寫吧。聽說荷蘭人自己有時候搞不清楚。
We made a special trip to the museum to see the Van Gogh.

法國姓的字首小寫。
Guy de Maupassant
Charles de Galle

義大利姓的字首大寫。
Andrea Della Robbia

西班牙很複雜：
Bartolomé de Las Casas

畢加索的全名是 Pablo Diego José Francisco de Paula Juan Nepomuceno María de los Remedios Cipriano de la Santísima Trinidad Ruiz y Picasso，記都記不得，還一堆大小寫，難怪他不走文字路線！咱們不管這些，好嗎？

Capitalize and punctuate these sentences.

❶ bartholomew wanted to buy two tickets to the ariana grande concert because he really wanted to hear her sing thank u next but they were sold out by the time he went online

❷ nascar the national association for stock car auto racing was founded in 1948 by bill big bill france sr

❸ cohl furey will be discussing mathematics and elementary particles at dr dattas office tomorrow afternoon but im afraid i wont have a chance to talk with her

❹ you ought to consider integrating zoom and slack if your team uses slack to communicate in real time just type /zoom into slack and join the meeting link which appears

❺ during the 2020 coronavirus crisis bored hunger games fans sectioned the united states off into separate districts sparking debate about the size of district eleven

參考例句

❶ Bartholomew wanted to buy two tickets to the Ariana Grande concert because he really wanted to hear her sing Thank U, Next, but they were sold out by the time he went online.

❷ NASCAR (the National Association for Stock Car Auto Racing) was founded in 1948 by Bill (Big Bill) France Sr.

❸ Cohl Furey will be discussing mathematics and elementary particles at Dr Datta's office tomorrow afternoon, but I'm afraid I won't have a chance to talk with her.

❹ You ought to consider integrating Zoom and Slack if your team uses Slack to communicate in real time; just type "/zoom" into Slack and join the meeting link which appears.

❺ During the 2020 coronavirus crisis, bored Hunger Games fans sectioned the United States off into separate districts, sparking debate about the size of District Eleven.

Practice writing

Complete these sentences. Try not to write something obvious. Think a bit.

The pickpocket silently __________

An elephant's ears __________

The truck quickly pulled into the parking space Bethany wanted, so __________

The movie was so boring that ____________________

The general chuckled when he saw ____________________

Write a sentence for each of these words.

- stand
- charge
- bagpipes
- sophisticated
- sycophant

Write an essay.

Do you think high school students should wear uniforms to school? Explain your standpoint and your reasoning.

Now write the essay from the opposing standpoint.

▶▶ Chapter 13 字型心理學：每款功效大不同

My dear sweetheart, I am looking forward to seeing you! It's been three days since I last saw you, and I can't get you out of my mind. (Times New Roman)

My dear sweetheart, I am looking forward to seeing you! It's been three days since I last saw you, and I can't get you out of my mind. (BlackChancery)

My dear sweetheart, I am looking forward to seeing you! It's been three days since I last saw you, and I can't get you out of my mind. (THICKER)

My dear sweetheart, I am looking forward to seeing you! It's been three days since I last saw you, and I can't get you out of my mind. (Ipadfont)

四段內容一樣；效果相同嗎？

假如到銀行、保險公司求職，and you write in a font like this，誰放心讓你處理財產？
本書重點在于寫作表達，但文章的視覺效果不可忽視；呈現的字體需要慎選，因為字型傳達很多訊息。

第一要訣：寫 abc 千萬不可用中文字型！！

好，知道了。可是選甚麼字型？先問，寫作的目的、風格、性質如何？
文章輕快、嚴肅、正式、親切，下筆求甚麼效果？

回到剛說的，到銀行、律師事務所、保險公司求職，要選比較保守的字型，如 Georgia、Cambria、Bell MT、Palatino，都很耐看。

Georgia, quiet geese and noisy turkeys.

Cambria, quiet geese and noisy turkeys.

Bell MT, quiet geese and noisy turkeys.

Palatino, quiet geese and noisy turkeys.

還有很多選擇，例如：

Plantagenet Cherokee, quiet geese and noisy turkeys.

Imperial BT, quiet geese and noisy turkeys.

Bodoni 72, quiet geese and noisy turkeys.

Iowan Old Style, quiet geese and noisy turkeys.

Didot, quiet geese and noisy turkeys.

Lucida Bright, quiet geese and noisy turkeys.

Athelas, quiet geese and noisy turkeys.

Berling Roman, quiet geese and noisy turkeys.

Garamond, quiet geese and noisy turkeys.

Bookman Old Style, quiet geese and noisy turkeys.

這些字型都很穩重、文雅。如果要強調頭腦很呆板、沒有美感、不願掌握人生，務必依據 Word 預設的 Times New Roman。

很多學刊規定用 Times New Roman，因為學術著作不許有美感。投稿，只好依照規定。

如果不需要繃著臉看的文章，可選比較俐落的字型。

Lexend Deca, wise gorillas and lighthearted pandas.

Incised901 Lt BT, wise gorillas and lighthearted pandas.

Lucida Sans, wise gorillas and lighthearted pandas.

Euphemia UCAS, wise gorillas and lighthearted pandas.

ITC Novarese STD Medium, wise gorillas and lighthearted pandas.

Optima, wise gorillas and lighthearted pandas.

Franklin Gothic Book, wise gorillas and lighthearted pandas.

Skia, wise gorillas and lighthearted pandas.

Artifica, wise gorillas and lighthearted pandas.

Candara, wise gorillas and lighthearted pandas.

有兩種字型，很多人感冒；本猩沒那麼討厭：

Comic Sans MS, fretting peacocks and considerate elephants.

Calibri, fretting peacocks and considerate elephants.

若要強調創意、文化、趣味，可選

Ipadfont, happy monkeys and serious butterflies.

Black Chancery, happy monkeys and serious butterflies.

Dalelands, happy monkeys and serious butterflies.

Friz Quadrata, happy monkeys and serious butterflies.

Luminari, happy monkeys and serious butterflies.

Gorilla, happy monkeys and serious butterflies.

Trattello, happy monkeys and serious butterflies.

Bulgaria Moderna V3, happy monkeys and serious butterflies.

上列創意字型未必適合長篇，但點綴就很活潑、討好。

各位，網路上可以下載千百種免費字型，不要客氣！請認真比較各種字型，慎選。當然要看個人審美觀。

文章稍長，建議選擇上列 Georgia、Cambria 等系列，或 Lexend；開發 Lexend 的團隊宣稱此字型最容易讀、提高讀者閱讀速度與吸收、減輕讀者眼睛的負擔。上網查 lexend.com，可以免費下載各種 Lexend 字型；本猩認為 Lexend Deca 適中，但因需而異。若字點數 (pt) 不高，Bodoni、Didot 不適合長篇，但標題、篇名、地址，就很適合。Bell MT、Garamond 字型很漂亮，而稍小，可憐讀者的眼睛，放大一點；注意行距。Euphemia UCAS 有點輕，若寫長篇，要留意視覺效果。

認識字型

大凡，字型兩類：serifs, sans serifs。
襯線體、無襯線體。何謂 serif ？字型末端的裝飾筆畫（如圖所圈為 serifs）

serif
sans-serif

Lucida Fax is a font that uses serifs.
Lucida Sans is a font that has no serifs.

Sans，法文，「無」，所以 sans serif 表示沒有襯線體。

一般較長的文章，用 serifs 多；電腦螢幕，似乎 sans serifs 容易讀。

Serifs 看起來稍微正式；sans serifs，反此。

二〇〇八年，Obama 競選總統，考慮 Hillary Clinton 文選用的 New Baskerville 字型，所以打算用 Perpetua 字型排版。競選團隊新加入的設計師，想煥然一新，選了剛發表的 Gotham 字型，俐落有勁，一砲而紅。問題是從此 Gotham 大紅大紫，可能太常用。斟酌用途、想達到的效果。

二〇二〇大選，字型公司專門為 Biden 設計了兩種新字型，Decimal 與 Mercury，美觀有力。Biden 當選了，字型非無功勞。

本猩喜歡乾淨利落、有個性的字型。網路上可以免費下載的字型很多，不要拘限于 Times New Roman；讀者可以了解 Sabon、Caslon、Bona Nova 甚至 LHF Encore，都很美。

無論選哪種字型，千萬記得，寫 abc 不可用中文字型！

特殊需求要考慮特別字型。例如，dyslexia（失讀症或閱讀障礙）患者不容易辨認一般字母，所以 OpenDyslexic 的設計使讀症患者輕鬆地閱讀。需要者上網免費下載字型。

Lesson III
高階語法與應用

Chapter 14 對稱法：用來美化文章 Good Things Come in Pairs

一九六一年，John F Kennedy 總統就職典禮演講說，Let every nation know, whether it wishes us well or ill, that we shall pay any price, bear any burden, meet any hardship, support any friend, oppose any foe to assure the survival and the success of liberty.

連續五個動詞 pay, bear, meet, support, oppose 不好寫；寫不好，語氣不暢、結構瑣碎、落為流水帳。合在一句，有節奏、有力量。文學素養高的人下筆才能如此。

二〇〇九年，Barack Obama 總統就職典禮演講說，My fellow citizens: I stand here today humbled by the task before us, grateful for the trust you have bestowed, mindful of the sacrifices borne by our ancestors. 連續三個形容詞 humbled, grateful, mindful，承接主詞動詞 I stand here，句子簡潔有力、優雅順暢。從 I 立即轉為 us、our，也是高筆。

英文的 parallel structure，亦稱 parallelism，讓文章容易了解，結構與文法完美，文筆優美，寫的好則更緊湊。句子容易了解、容易記得，文章對稱平衡，節奏宜人、悅耳，說服力增強。不宜太常用，當恰到好處：不要把英文寫成駢體文，但散文、詩、演講、論文、報告都適合；情書，更不用說了。

Parallel structure 容易記又順口，所以常用。

Love me, love my dog.

Easy come, easy go.

文學作品不乏 **parallel structure**。

Alexander Pope (1688 – 1744), *Essay on Criticism*：

To err is human, to forgive divine.

William Thackeray (1811 – 1863), *Vanity Fair* 一句結構很特別，

Think what right you have to be scornful, whose virtue is a deficiency of temptation, whose success may be a chance, whose rank may be an ancestor's accident, whose posterity is very likely a satire. 連用四個 whose 修飾 you，瞧不起他人的人。

Parallel structure 優美自有節奏，容易動人。請把 Dr Martin Luther King Jr 的名言念出來。

If it falls your lot to be a street sweeper, sweep streets like Michelangelo painted pictures, sweep streets like Beethoven composed music, sweep streets like Leontyne Price sings before the Metropolitan Opera. Sweep streets like Shakespeare wrote poetry. Sweep streets so well that all the hosts of heaven and earth will have to pause and say: Here lived a great street sweeper who did his job well.

他舉 sweep streets，略嫌繞口，但二字說出來，二長母音相應，似用力將掃帚來回掃之音。

英文寫作的 parallel structure，類似中文的對句：飛龍乘雲、騰蛇遊霧。（韓非子難勢引慎子）飛對騰、龍對蛇、乘對遊、雲對霧。這種寫法美，又讓人印象深刻。但寫英文很重要的一點是，句型、時態要一致。例如，

Guo had a free weekend. He went to the seashore. At the seashore, he went diving. He put on his scuba gear carefully. He tested everything. Then he got into the water. He slowly dived deeper into the water. He admired all the fish and the coral. He took many photographs.

這種寫法太呆板，氣不順，很難捉住讀者的興趣。串起來吧：
On a free weekend, Guo went to the seashore to go diving. He put on his scuba gear carefully, tested everything, got into the water, and slowly dove deeper, admiring and photographing all the fish and the coral.

時態都一致。下文是錯誤示範：
On a free weekend, Guo went to the seashore to go diving. He put on his scuba gear carefully, testing everything, getting into the water, and slowly dove deeper, admired and photographed all the fish and the coral. 💣

可寫作：
On a free weekend, Guo went to the seashore to go diving. He put on his scuba gear carefully, testing everything getting into the water, and slowly dove deeper, admiring and photographing all the fish and the coral.

意思不太一樣：好像同時帶上潛水裝備，並且測試而且下水。

寫：

On a free weekend, Guo went to the seashore to go diving. He put on his scuba gear carefully, testing everything, got into the water, and slowly dove deeper, admiring and photographing all the fish and the coral.

表示邊帶上裝備邊測試。但依照原來一堆句子，好像有先後，所以這樣寫不太一樣。但此句寫法不佳，因為 put 過去式 + testing 動詞型態不同 Ving + got 過去式 + dove 過去式。不是很順。最後的 admiring and photographing 沒有問題，因為是句尾綴詞。

看看還有甚麼樣的 parallel structure 可以用。

- **to V** 可以串

  Britany likes to hike. She likes to sail. She likes to play badminton.

  Britany likes to hike, to sail, and to play badminton.

  Britany likes to hike, sail, and play badminton.

  Britany likes to hike, to sail, and play badminton. 💣

  Britany likes to hike, to sail, and playing badminton. 💣

- **Ving** 也可以串

  Britany likes hiking, sailing, and playing badminton.

  Britany likes hiking, sailing, and badminton. 差強人意。

  Britany likes hiking, sailing, and enjoys badminton. 💣

  Britany likes hiking, sailing, and to play badminton. 💣

- 副詞可以疊

  The accountant worked quickly. The accountant worked accurately. The accountant worked carefully.

The accountant worked quickly, accurately, and carefully.

- **either or**

You may choose to either have this one repaired or buy a new one. 💣

You may choose to either have this one repaired or to buy a new one. 💣

You may choose either to have this one repaired or to buy a new one. 尚可。

You may choose either to have this one repaired or buy a new one. 💣

許多評論家認為 neither nor 不合時代、做作。見仁見智。

- **not only A, but B**

最基本型態是 not only A, but B，不止 A 並且還有 B，重點在 B。可以增加：

not only A, but also B

not only A, but B as well

not only A, but also B as well

後面越加，B 的份量越重。但現今美國人往往太省，寫 not only A, B，連 but 也省，這太省。

She came to the party. She brought cookies. She brought tortilla chips, too.

She brought not only cookies to the party, but tortilla chips as well.

She not only brought cookies to the party, but tortilla chips as well. 💣

> 一般華語背景的人寫英文，需要特別注意時態、單複數、verb agreement。

The class discussed the movie. They discussed the book. The movie was based on the book.
The class discussed not only the movie, but also the book it was based on.
The class discussed not only the movie, but also the book on which it was based.
The class discussed not only the movie, but the book also which it was based on. 💣

有人規定句子最後一個字不可以用介系詞收尾。本猩無所謂。

The class discussed the movie. They wrote reviews on the movie.
They not only discussed the movie, but also wrote reviews.
They not only discussed the movie, but also wrote reviews on it.
They not only discussed the movie, but also they wrote reviews. 💣
They not only discussed the movie, but reviews. 💣

Tayal warriors surrendered. Japanese soldiers slaughtered them. The Japanese soldiers slaughtered children who had done nothing wrong.
Japanese soldiers slaughtered not only Tayal warriors who had surrendered, but also innocent children as well.

懂了嗎？自己練習看看！

Combine these words into sentences.

Use no redundant words.

1. Sharon / bought / new smartphone / battery bank / wireless earphones
2. they tasted / coffee / brazil / guatamala / ethiopia / finally / settled / yellow honey process / uraga / ethiopia / grown / altitudes / 2021 / 2096 meters / best

Uraga，烏拉嘎。

3. Jennifer / speaks/ not only / English / but also / Swedish / Finnish / Russian
4. movie / long / that / we / ate / all / popcorn / finished / soft drinks / got hungry / again
5. soldier / jumped / out / plane / shouted Geronimo / pulled / ripcord / made sure / parachute / opened / slowly / floated / earth

Geronimo (1829 – 1909) 是美國西南著名的 Apache 族驍勇戰士；英勇無比，所以美軍傘兵跳傘時，喊 Geronimo，紀念勇士、給自己打氣，喊完開降落傘時間剛好。

參考例句

❶ **Sharon bought a new smartphone, a new battery bank, and wireless earphones.**

評：兩個耳朵，所以 earphones 複數。

❷ **They tasted coffee from Brazil, Guatamala, and Ethiopia, and finally settled on yellow honey process coffee from Uraga in Ethiopia – grown at altitudes of 2021 to 2096 meters – as the best.**

評：國名、地名要大寫。
海拔片語前後亦可加括弧，但本猩認為連字號比較不突兀。

❸ **Jennifer speaks not only English, but also Swedish, Finnish, and Russian.**

❹ **The movie was so long that we ate all of our popcorn, finished our soft drinks, and got hungry again.**

❺ **The soldier jumped out of the plane, shouted Geronimo, pulled the ripcord, made sure the parachute opened, and slowly floated to the earth.**

Combine these sentences.

Write economically.

1. I woke up in the morning. It was Monday. I saw that it was raining. I muttered under my breath. I got dressed. I prepared to leave. I was going to the office.
2. Somebody betrayed the Mafia boss. There were only two people who could have betrayed him. It might have been Salvatore, and it might have been Vincent.
3. Alexis looked in the park. She looked up and down the street. She looked in the mall. She looked in the school. She looked for her beagle. Her beagle was named Fido. Fido had run after a squirrel. Fido had not come back yet.
4. When they enter prison, inmates may possess only certain items, and those items have to be approved when they are admitted to the prison. They may also possess items which the prison staff have issued to them. They may possess things if they buy them from the prison commissary. If the inmates buy or receive items, they may keep some of them, but only if they came through approved channels.
5. We need fiber in our diet. Sometimes we get very, very much cholesterol in our body and we need something to clean that cholesterol up and get it out of our body, or else we will get much cholesterol in our body. Otherwise it goes into our arteries and that is very bad so we need fiber. We can get fiber from sesame. That is very good for us.

參考例句

❶ **When I woke up on Monday morning and saw that it was raining, I muttered under my breath as I got dressed and prepared to leave for the office.**

評：Dressed 後可加逗點，但不必。Leave N，離開 N; leave for N，出發往 N。

❷ **Either Salvatore or Vincent betrayed the Mafia boss.**

❸ **Alexis looked in the park, up and down the street, in the mall, and in the school for her beagle, Fido, which had run after a squirrel and not come back yet.**

評：Which 可改 who，強調愛犬的人性。

❹ **Upon entering prison, inmates may possess only certain items approved on admission, items issued by prison staff, items bought from the prison commissary, or items bought or received through approved channels.**

評：為了寫很清楚、排除疑問或爭執，不妨重複 items.

❺ **Sesame provides a good source for dietary fiber, which sops up extra cholesterol in your system and removes it before it clogs up your arteries.**

評：「我們」不等于 we；英文的 we 限定範圍，某一群人。若寫 we need fiber in our diet，很容易誤會，只有一部分的人有此需求。事實上，所有人需要纖維，因此正確、現代的英文用 you。古人往往用 one，表示中立，但文法很容易打結；現代人看不習慣。

Improve these sentences.

1. The skill of English writing of myself is getting better slow but sure.
2. Firefighters are required to respond quickly, putting out fire, to help maybe some people need help.
3. As per the impact of very, very old, very conventional manner"Sanskrit" drama, it has been since the 1970's, multiple "Bollywood" movies they put together a lot of action and some very funny stuff and maybe somebody falls in love. and its gorgeous and phenomenal to look at. and sometimes very serious and this film now people call it MASALA film as seen in aforementioned "Bollywood" movies
4. The Duesenberg Special was built in 1935 on a Duesenberg Model J rolling chassis, and it had a modified front axle, as well as a standard wheelbase, in addition to a non-standard high rear axle ratio.
5. Fashionable gurus urge you to "follow your passion," but if you do that, you might end up on a slippery slope and then you will be prey to anxiety and depression, and in the end you very possibly will burn out.

參考例句

1. **My English writing skill is improving slowly but surely.**

評：Slowly 毋加逗點。

2. **Firefighters are required to respond quickly, put out fires, and help those who need assistance.**

評：為何 help 改 assistance？為了避免重複 help。為何第一 help 不改 assist？因為 help 字短、有勁；help 起自日耳曼語，assist 起自拉丁文。

❸ **Influenced by ancient stylized Sanskrit drama, since the 1970s, many Bollywood movies freely mix action, comedy, romance, spectacle, and drama in a style called the masala film.**

評：本猩不是開玩笑的，要寫作要多背單字。
也要分辨。Impact（名詞）指具體的撞擊，如石頭滾下山撞地。此句宜改 influence。
刪除不必要的、傷眼的引號、大寫。但要記得用 Oxford comma。
不要寫 as per、aforementioned。

❹ **Built in 1935 on a Duesenberg Model J rolling chassis, the Duesenberg Special had a modified front axle, a standard wheelbase, and a non-standard high rear axle ratio.**

❺ **Following your passion as fashionable gurus urge could very well send you down a slippery slope leading to anxiety, depression, and ultimately burnout.**

Practice Writing

Complete these sentences. Use your imagination.

During his short career, ________

The crowd rushed forward to see ________

A large seagull ________

The sign by the side of the road ________________

At the most lonesome time of dusk, ________________

Write a sentence for each of these words.

- ignore
- crop
- involved
- sloop
- augment

Write an essay.

Some people say that before long, all cars will be self-driving. Do you agree or disagree? What are the advantages and disadvantages of self-driving cars?

Now write the essay from the opposing viewpoint.

Chapter 15 嵌入句：併句長話短說
Russian Dolls

中文的特點之一，較少嵌入子句、句子。You may have noticed that something unusual about Chinese is that embedded sentences are seldom used. 遑論寫作，此類句型在英語口頭上十分常用，而依我教學經驗來看，臺灣學生很少用。

兩句合爲一句，最簡單的型態，將問句嵌入直述句。注意字詞順序！
Is he busy? Ask him. → Ask him if he is busy.
When will he be free? Ask him. → Ask him when he will be free.

這種用法在口頭上十分普遍，而在寫作更可以發揮。
Their dog is very friendly. Its name is Fido. It licked my face. It wagged its tail.

口語變化不大。
Their dog Fido is really friendly. It licked my face and wagged its tail.

書寫可以拾綴。
Wagging its tail, their friendly dog Fido licked my face.
Their friendly dog Fido, wagging its tail, licked my face.

亦可寫 Their friendly dog Fido licked my face as it wagged its tail，然 it 後接 its，略拙。Licking my face, their friendly dog Fido wagged its tail，亦可，而重點稍異。

Josh felt tired. He put his head on his desk. He took a nap.
這三句，很直很硬。口語的說法：
Josh felt tired so he put his head on his desk and took a nap.

寫作可以潤飾：
Josh, who felt tired, put his head on his desk and took a nap.
Josh, feeling tired, put his head on his desk for a nap.
Feeling tired, Josh put his head on his desk for a nap.

嵌入句示範

Brian was dirty. He had played soccer. The field was muddy. He looked forward to taking a shower. He wanted a nice shower that was hot.

口語表達

Brian was dirty from playing soccer on a muddy field, so he looked forward to a nice, hot shower.

書寫表達

❶ Brian, dirty from playing soccer on a muddy field, looked forward to a nice, hot shower.
❷ Dirty from playing soccer on a muddy field, Brian looked forward to a nice, hot shower.
❸ The prospect of a nice, hot shower appealed to Brian, as he was dirty from playing soccer on a muddy field.
❹ The prospect of a nice, hot shower appealed to Brian, dirty from playing soccer on a muddy field.

句子不宜過長，但嵌入法可以串若干短句。

The rain was pelting down. Thunder rolled. Sarah held her umbrella high. It didn't do any good. She raced from her car to the door. The door led into the department store. 合寫：

Racing from her car to the department store door, Sarah held her useless umbrella high as rain pelted down and thunder rolled.
Holding her useless umbrella high against the pelting rain and rolling thunder, Sarah raced from her car to the door of the department store.

注意嵌入句必須配合前動詞的時態。

She is ready，是現在式，但是嵌入 She phoned to tell me，phoned 是過去式，所以通常寫：She phoned to tell that me that she was ready.

現在用法，往往保留後句的時態：She phoned to tell me that she is ready. 雖不算極好，可以接受；用法要一致。

中間用 **that** 連接，通常可以省略。

She phoned to tell me she was ready.

如果少了 **that** 句意不明，一定要加。

They decided that that one was too expensive.

That 有兩種發音。
當代名詞、形容詞、副詞，讀 [ðæt]，
當連接詞讀 [ðət]，通常可以省略。

如果只寫 They decided that one was too expensive，讀者不清楚是 that one 特定的那個，或者 one 某一個。

也要聽句子的節奏。
The service center informed us that the website would be unavailable from 9AM to 3PM on Sunday. 此句如果不留 that，us 直連 the website，節奏嫌峻峭，還是保留較好。

當然，說「節奏峻峭」，很主觀。如何培養這種主觀呢？多多閱讀、多多寫作、用心聽。

怎麼救呢？拿出大刀來，揮起斧頭來，砍！

Combine the following sentences.

Yes/no questions

1. Is there a doctor on the plane? The flight attendant asked.
2. Does Hannah know how to ski? Sarah wanted to find out before the trip.
3. Did she gain weight over the holidays? Anita tried not to find out.
4. Will the flight be on time? The passenger asked the lady at the airline counter. He asked her many times. This was the sixth time.
5. Does Brianna want black sesame on her noodles? Does Brianna want white sesame on her noodles? Find out.

參考例句

現在口語多用 if，whether 較為加強語氣。寫作都可以。
下列參考例句，本猩懶得打 whether，所以用 if，兩者均可。

❶ **The flight attendant asked if there was a doctor on the plane.**

❷ **Before the trip, Sarah wanted to find out if Hannah knew how to ski.**

❸ **Anita tried not to find out if she gained weight over the holidays.**

❹ **For the sixth time, the passenger asked the lady at the airline counter if the flight would be on time.**

評：若寫 The passenger asked the lady at the airline counter for the sixth time if the flight would be on time，似乎地勤人員第六次在櫃台。寫 The passenger asked the lady at the airline counter if the flight would be on time for the sixth time，似乎問班次是否第六次準時。

❺ **Find out if Brianna wants black or white sesame on her noodles.**

本猩看過這麼一句：
She asked whether weather was a factor in their decision.
我的媽咪呀！

Information questions

1. How much coffee do we have left? I need to know.
2. How much coffee did we have left? I needed to know.
3. How big is Lake Michigan? Natalie was wondering. She was flying across it.
4. He dropped out of school. He was a senior. He was supposed to graduate in only four months. His father wanted to know the reason.
5. It has been raining for a long time. It may keep raining for a long time. He asked me if I knew.
6. The manager put his notes somewhere, but he's not sure where. The notes are for the meeting. He will have a meeting with the Board. His assistant reminded him.

參考例句

❶ **I need to know how much coffee we have left.**

❷ **I needed to know how much coffee we had left.**

❸ **Natalie was wondering how big Lake Michigan was while she was flying across it.**
Flying across Lake Michigan, Natalie was wondering how big it was.

評：Lake Michigan 面積不變，但為了配合前面 was wondering 的過去進行式，所以最好用 was，不用 is。

❹ **His father wanted to know why he dropped out of school in his senior year, only four months from graduation.**
His father wanted to know the reason he dropped out of school in his senior year, only four months from graduation.

評：美國人也會寫 the reason why，但邏輯不通：the reason 才對。

❺ **He asked me if I knew how long it would keep raining.**

❻ **The manager's assistant reminded him where he put his notes for the meeting with the board.**

Combine these sentences.

1. He admitted. He is wrong.
2. The performance begins soon. We will be late. It is quite likely.
3. Austin wrote to me. He is going to finish his thesis before long. His thesis is about the nutritional value of sesame oil.
4. Isaiah got off the bus. He left his laptop on his seat in the bus. He realized that.
5. That is the best way to solve the problem. That is what we think.

洛杉磯商店招牌

Our motto is to give our customers the lowest possible prices and workmanship.

怎麼改呢？想一想。

參考例句

下列參考句，that 當介系詞，均可省。依字句節奏增減。

❶ **He admitted that he was wrong.**

❷ **It is quite likely that we will be late for the performance.**

❸ **Austin wrote me that he was going to finish his thesis about the nutritional value of sesame oil before long.**
Austin wrote me that before long he was going to finish his thesis about the nutritional value of sesame oil.

評：相同內容靠攏：請參考 Chapter 23，訣竅三：集合相關字。因為 thesis 修飾語多，before long 吊車尾，讀者乍以為 finish 而已，突然冒出 before long，思緒擾亂。不如將 before long 向前挪。

❹ **After Isaiah got off the bus, he realized that he had left his laptop on his seat in the bus.**

❺ **We thought that that was the best way to solve the problem.**

評：口頭上，二 that 音不同。

Practice Writing

Complete these sentences. Use your imagination. Try not to write something obvious.

She hadn't eaten since ________________

The other team will reciprocate when ________________

At the station, a blind lady asked ________________

His hair looked like ________________

As the oven exploded, ________________

Write a sentence for each of these words. If possible, develop them into complete essays. Keep your sentences strong and lithe. Prefer active verbs. Use words that are appropriate for the reader.

- proud
- cover
- heresy
- convulsion
- recover

Write an essay.

Write about a time you were lost.

Chapter 16 修飾語：沒排對會引起誤會

Dangling Particles.

我們已經練過將子句、片語加到句中；現在要練習省略，要確定文法通，修飾語沒排錯。Native speakers 也容易犯這種錯，所以笑話很多。下列幾句都是美國人寫的。看得出問題嗎？

After sitting on the shelf for some months, I finally took down the book and started reading. 💣

來看看吧。Ving 片語啟後省略，主詞必須一致。假若不一致，省略語不修飾主詞，英文叫做 dangling particles；娛樂價值雖高，但語意不清楚。

「我在架子上坐了好幾個月之後，才把書拿下來看。」怎麼改呢？

After it had been sitting on the shelf for some months, I finally took down the book and started reading.

After the book had been sitting on the shelf for some months, I finally took it down and started reading.

若寫

I finally took the book down after it had been sitting on the shelf for some months and started reading，尚可，但 took 與 reading 離的稍遠，讀者不容易連貫。

Driving like a maniac, the deer was killed as it crossed the road. 💣 我沒看過鹿開車呢！

Some maniac driver killed the deer as it crossed the road.
As it crossed the road, the deer was killed by someone driving like a maniac.

Having finished the main course, the waiter offered to serve dessert. 💣 服務到家！服務生還幫忙吃主菜！
After I finished the main course, the waiter offered to serve dessert.
The waiter offered to serve dessert after I had finished the main course.

有時候，整句話要改。
Wagging his tail happily, my husband walked our dog through the park. 💣
要改
Our dog wagged his tail happily as my husband walked him through the park. 除非妳老公有尾巴。

Melting under the hot sun, Jennifer quickly finished her ice cream cone. 💣
Jennifer quickly finished her ice cream cone because it was melting under the hot sun.

懂了嗎？自己多練習。

Improve these sentences.

❶ Covered with chocolate chips, I enjoyed the cookies.

❷ Working on her computer, the cat jumped into Amber's lap.

❸ While eating breakfast, an elephant approached our camp.

❹ After years of being lost under a pile of dust, Isaac found the box of photographs.

❺ Stuck in a long line of cars, traffic was so heavy that Ariana almost missed her flight.

參考例句

❶ **I enjoyed the cookies covered with chocolate chips.**

❷ **While Amber was working on her computer, her cat jumped into her lap.**

❸ **An elephant approached our camp while we were eating breakfast.**
While we were eating breakfast, an elephant approached our camp.

❹ **Isaac found the box of photographs which had been lost under a pile of dust for years.**

❺ **Traffic was so heavy that Ariana, stuck in a long line of cars, almost missed her flight.**
Stuck in a long line of cars, Ariana almost missed her flight.

評：Stuck in a long line of cars，理所當然是 heavy traffic，不必贅述。第二句略勝。

Hopefully 的用法

Hopefully 這個副詞怎麼用？本猩從不用。嚴格說，Hopefully, the weather will be good tomorrow 屬于 dangling particle，文法通俗但不通。

一則副詞該少用，一則敢抱希望，就要勇敢說出是誰希望：who hopes the weather will be good tomorrow? 不敢貼出主詞，就不要抱希望唄。直說無礙。

Practice Writing

Complete these sentences. Use your imagination.

As the rising sun dimmed the stars, ____________________

The sailors on the sinking boat saw a freighter ____________________

The octopus said to the elephant, ____________________

Three men stood by the door __________

Hot coffee ____________________

Write a sentence for each of these words.

- Incredible
- calamity
- unreliable
- nonchalant
- gem

Write an essay.

Write about something funny that happened to you in high school.

Remember to use the past tense. Give details, tell a story.

Chapter 17 倒裝句：強化重點 Topsy-turvy Sentences

通常英文的排列是：主詞＋動詞＋受詞＋介系詞片語，但句子依需可以變化：為了讓文章更通順、容易了解、增強變化、強調，可以倒裝句。

I talked to a woman who was born in Botswana in the workshop.
這樣寫，不清楚她在工作坊裏的波札那生的？在波札那的工作坊裏生？
調位置：In the workshop, I talked to a woman who was born in Botswana. 意思就明白。

We had never seen anything like it.
句子弱。
Never had we seen anything like it.

I realized my neighbor was an opera singer when I saw him on the stage.
可以更生動：
Not until I saw the him on the stage did I realize that my neighbor was an opera singer.

可以這樣寫：
First you have to pay back the money. Finley won't tear up your IOU before then. 但可以強調：
First you have to pay back the money. Only then will Finley tear up your IOU.

Ryan slammed on the brakes when he realized that the car in front of him had stopped.

可以加強：

Only when Ryan realized the car in front of him had stopped did he slam on the brakes.

Invert these sentences.

1. You will find the apple sauce I bought for you in the back of the refrigerator.
2. The soldiers snapped to attention as soon as the general stood on the reviewing platform.
3. Jonathan did not imagine that his carelessness would have such grave repercussions.
4. So many flamingoes had never gathered in the park across the road before.
5. Paper mulberry trees, which originated in Taiwan, grow throughout the Pacific region.

paper mulberry, *Broussonetia papyrifera*, 構樹。

參考例句

❶ **In the back of the refrigerator you will find the apple sauce I bought for you.**

評：In the back of the refrigerator，在冰箱最裏面；in back of the refrigerator，在冰箱的外面，在後面。

❷ **No sooner had the general stood on the reviewing platform than the soldiers snapped to attention.**

❸ **Little did Jonathan imagine that his carelessness would have such grave repercussions.**

❹ **Never before had so many flamingoes gathered in the park across the road.**

❺ **Throughout the Pacific region grow paper mulberry trees, which originated in Taiwan.**

評：若無逗點，originated in Taiwan 修飾 paper mulberry trees，表示太平洋地區有些構樹來自臺灣，有些來自其它區域，而太平洋的構樹，全由臺灣散播。因此，逗點不可或缺。

Improve these sentences.

❶ Turboshaft aircraft engines are used on helicopters commonly, and the turboshaft engine is very much like turbojet engine howsoever the former has a large shaft which connect front and back,

❷ In Uruguay have largest salt plan on Earth, name is Lake Uyuni, is 130 kilometers from side to side and very, very flat, the skies is very, very clear, so it is very good for the calibration of Earth observation satellites' altimeters.

❸ The teacher perceived that the student displayed an attitude of enthusiasm for multiple musical instruments of the Renaissance period of time, such as the recorder, the shawm, the sackbut... etc.

❹ Have one coffeehouse in London, name Lloyd's Coffeehouse, that year 1686, sea captains gather there for coffee, merchants gather there, too, and sailor, too, and they all mention about shipping informations and many ships sink but some come to port without dangerous,so the people there they start to gamble.they put down bet on which ship come to poat without dangerous、now is very famous insrnce market name Lloy'd of London and this is how he start

❺ Leprechauns are very small supernatural beings in the myths which come from Ireland and make much mischief and are very, very greedy, and hide their gold in pots and hide the pots at the end of rainbows

參考例句

❶ **Commonly used on helicopters, turboshaft engines are similar to turbojets, but have a large shaft connecting the front to the back.**

評：句點，不是逗點。

❷ **The largest salt pan on this planet, Lake Uyuni in Bolivia is 130 kilometers across, exceptionally flat, and enjoys clear skies, making it ideal for calibrating the altimeters of Earth observation satellites.**

評：逗點不可置行首。
寫作要謹慎：Lake Uyuni 在 Bolivia，不在 Uruguay。

❸ **The teacher saw that the student was enthusiastic about Renaissance musical instruments such as the recorder, shawm, and sackbut.**

評：Renaissance 是時期，不必加 period；period 是時期，period of time 冗，刪。考慮前後文。假使全文討論音樂，可以刪 musical。

> such as 已說明舉例而已，不可加 etc，更不可畫三點。

❹ **In 1686, sailors, sea captains, and merchants gathering for coffee at Lloyd's Coffeehouse in London to discuss shipping started laying bets on which ships would arrive safely; this is the origin of the renowned insurance market, Lloyd's of London.**

評：Mention，順便提，後加受詞，不加 about；而此情形，mention 不當。

> Information 不可數，沒有加 s 的道理。
> 注意標點的用法、空格。英文不可用頓號。

❺ **Diminutive supernatural beings in Irish mythology, leprechauns are avaricious mischief-makers who cache their gold in pots which they hide at the end of rainbows.**

> Things done fast disappear fast; only what is done with time will remain.
>
> 攝影大師／ Henri Cartier-Bresson

Practice Writing

Complete these sentences. Let your imagination fly. See what you can come up with.

Inside his castle, the knight ________________

The most bizarre person at the party ________________

On a recent shopping expedition ________

By irritating his father, ________________

The strong tropical sunlight ________________

Write a sentence for each of these words.

- intrigue
- strut
- truculent
- glance
- register

Write an essay.

We mentioned the paper mulberry, 構樹 , spread from Taiwan throughout the Pacific. Why did the voyagers take this tree with them? What was valuable about it? What did they use it for?

Chapter 18 選字訣竅：先動詞後名詞
Make Sentences More Powerful

語言本質是口說，寫作不得違犯口語。我相信讀者不會跟親朋好友說：
我在即將來臨的時間裏要加以購買一杯咖啡。
哥哥在作掃客廳的動作中。
你對牙齒進行了洗刷部分的作業嗎？

而時下文章，贅字氾濫。何謂贅字？如果刪此字，字句一樣可通，刪！不要手軟！殺！

當然要慮及字句節奏、聲音和諧，但沒有作用的字眼，殺！

寫作是藝術，藝術就是爬羅剔抉，刮垢磨光。

Chapter 1 引 Strunk and White 要旨。這句，needless 有同義詞 unnecessary，怎麼選？ Unnecessary 四個音節、needless 兩個音節；要聽全句節奏、音律，但通常要選短字。短字緊湊、集中、有力；長字垮、力量分散。

若要考究，還有一層關係：need 來自日耳曼語，necessary 來自拉丁文；日耳曼語是英語的近親，所以其字親切、有勁。拉丁文是旁系親屬，用在英文，其字弱、垮。

煉字，能刪字尾就刪：
There was great excitement among the crowd.
Excitement，名詞，字尾 ment 可以刪：The crowd was excited.

Karen's advocacy for stricter regulations on supervisory positions has taken an increasingly antagonistic tone.

Advocacy 名詞，四音節，不如動詞 advocate，三音節。Regulation 名詞，不如動詞 regulate。Supervisory positions，囉唆，supervisors；嚴格說，需要 regulate 是 supervisor 本人，不是這個職位。An increasingly antagonistic tone，囉唆，不如多背單字，strident。Karen has become more strident as she advocates regulating supervisors more strictly.

刪字尾，必須保留本意。如 ignorant（愚）或 ignoramus（笨蛋）刪字尾，成為動詞 ignore（不理不睬），意思變了。

又如 advance、advancement，意思不同。Advance，名動兼用，指各方面的進步、進展、向前、預支薪資；現今許多英文程度不足的人將 advancement 等同 advance 的名詞，且不知，advancement 只有兩種正確的用法：職業晉升、推廣。

寫作謹慎、理路縝密的人比較在乎字用得貼切與否、意思表達清楚了沒？

例如，use 動名詞兼用，usage 專指字詞用法，意義不同，不可混淆！Utility 是實用、多用途。但有人從 utility 加上字尾 ize 變 utilize，意思與 use（動詞）無別，不需要存在；更而甚者，將 utilize 化成名詞，變 utilization，意思與 use（名詞）無別，又長了很多贅肉。

Sign 是招牌，英文有單複數，所以很多招牌、招牌類，加 s，天靈靈地靈靈，變！複數了！解決了。可是 signs，小孩子能講，有的人就寫成 signage，此字不必存在。

猶如天雨路滑，「滑」動詞 slip、slide，就很漂亮，歷史悠久又好聽。可是有人硬要用 hydroplane，三個音節拉丁字根取代一個音節日耳曼字，文學素養何在？諸如此類，不可取！

寫作著重以下順序：動詞、名詞、形容詞、副詞

- **Choose verbs first.**

先選動詞，因爲動詞動。偶用被動，可以，但勿常用。

They came to the decision that the event should be held on Tuesday.

They decided to hold the event on Tuesday.

She made a determination concerning their subsequent course of action.

She determined their next step.

需要斟酌。有的動詞不漂亮；避免太多 **ize** 或 **ify** 結尾的動詞。

The new design uglified the building. 真的是 ugly。

The new design made the building ugly.

The committee brought the plans to the final stage 若改為

The committee finalized the plans 現在雖然常見，但不漂亮。

The committee finished the plans.

有，可以捉模，無，是缺乏，所以肯定句比否定句有力。寫否定句，不如發揮字彙能力來取代多餘的否定句。

She thought his standpoint was not persuasive.

His standpoint was unpersuasive.

加強字彙。

The auditor had a feeling that there was not enough evidence, and made a decision not to investigate the parts where the books didn't look quite right.

The auditor felt the evidence was insufficient, and chose to ignore the irregularities in the books.

- **Nouns are concrete.**

名詞可以獨立站住腳，所以動詞配名詞。但英文名詞的缺點，invention, intention, intervention, retention, precipitation, anticipation, convention, realization 太多名詞 ion 結尾，用多了不好聽。

若有動詞可用，不要太多名詞。研究者往往串很多名詞，文筆呆滯難讀：confirmability, transferability, credibility，一堆名詞排在一串很悶。

動詞、名詞用完了才選形容詞，形容詞不夠用才把副詞派上場。

Write with nouns and verbs, not with adjectives and adverbs. The adjective hasn't been built that can pull a weak or inaccurate noun out of a tight place.

美國作家／ E. B. White

▪ Adjectives describe.

形容詞加味道。英文形容詞排列有固定的順序，但只要順序對，native speakers 完全不察覺。

若寫 an enamel, red, new mug，嚴格說沒有錯，但是讀起來十分不順。習慣的順序是 a new, red enamel mug。為甚麼？沒有為甚麼，語言是習慣，如此而已。

形容詞的順序是 quantity (number), size, quality (opinion), age, shape, color, origin, material, type, purpose：
They had three small, exquisite, old, round, white Chinese porcelain tea pots.

當然，不要那麼一串形容詞，但對 native speakers 來講，這樣才對。如果寫 They had white, Chinese, round, three exquisite tea pots，不至于招天譴，但很怪，好像哪裏脫軌了。寫者或許求特殊效果，但怕讀者分心，停下來咀嚼，這句哪裏怪？這不是我們要的。

▪ Adverbs are weak.

副詞重要，但副詞依附動詞，較弱，而英文副詞，如 quickly, hypothetically, affably, stubbornly, tiredly, comically, tragically, theoretically 多數 ly 結尾，聽多了會暈。

副詞依附動詞，所以加 ly, ly 副詞，不如慎選動詞。
He loudly called for them to move at a quicker speed.
He shouted for them to hurry.

Improve these sentences.

1. They sought and found a resolution to the predicament concerning the placement of the signage.
2. The assemblywoman exercised persuasion on the other members of the assembly to reach an agreement concerning the issue about which she had made a proposal.
3. At a meeting held by the staff to prioritize the items to be discussed at the once-a-year conference, there was no disagreement concerning the necessity of discussing the pension fund.
4. Exercising by means of the utilization of her limbs to achieve forward propulsion in an aquatic environment definitely and positively impacted her physical condition.
5. There were so many sentences in the article which were not necessary, and this made the writing seem not so strong.
6. Clark Gable; a previously famous American actor, he played in "Gone With the Wind", that was his most famous role; his third wife Carole Lombard killed air crash in 1942 (she was returning from a War Bond drive), thereupon Gable left from the MGM (the famous movie film studio) and he participated in the Army.

參考例句

❶ **They resolved the predicament about placing the signs.**

❷ **The assemblywoman persuaded the other members of the assembly to agree to her proposal.**

❸ **At a staff meeting to determine priorities for the annual conference agenda, there was unanimous support for a discussion on the pension fund.**

❹ **Swimming was good for her health.**

❺ **Numerous superfluous sentences weakened the article.**

評：現在很多人認為 multiple 聽起來很權威，但 multiple 正確意思帶「重複」、「複製」的意思。不如用 numerous；自信的狠角色就寫 many。

❻ **When Carole Lombard, the third wife of the famous american actor Clark Gable, noted for his role in *Gone with the Wind*, died in an air crash in 1942 as she was returning from a War Bond drive, Gable left the famous film studio MGM and joined the Army.**

評：Previously，從前；若寫 previously famous，從前有名，現在沒有名了；而 Gable 雖過世五十年，至今盡人皆知，所以刪 previously。需要說明某人有名，大概沒有名：孔子中外皆知，需要說「有名的孔子」嗎？考慮刪 famous。英文不能說 participated in the Army。

太多括弧，文意不順、版面凌亂。Thereupon 適用于法律文件。Movie 與 film 為同義詞，刪一。

此一句實在裝太多內容。斟酌：讀者難道不知道 MGM 是重量級 film studio ？

美國人想到 Clark Gable，立即聯想到 Gone with the Wind ／亂世佳人 (“Frankly, my dear, I don’t give a damn.”) 需要說明嗎？我們再寫寫看：When Carole Lombard, the third wife of Clark Gable, died in an air crash in 1942 when she was returning from a War Bond drive, Gable left MGM and joined the Army.

這樣就一口吃下去。可以再調：When Carole Lombard, the third wife of Clark Gable, died in an air crash in 1942 while returning from a War Bond drive, Gable left MGM and joined the Army.

若改 When Clark Gable’s third wife, Carole Lombard, died in an air crash in 1942 while returning from a War Bond drive, he left MGM and joined the Army，重點移到 Gable。斟酌前後文、要點，還可以調：Clark Gable left MGM and joined the Army when his third wife, Carole Lombard, died in an air crash in 1942 while returning from a War Bond drive. 甚至于，Lombard 是第幾任妻子，那麼重要嗎？考慮刪 third。When Clark Gable’s wife, Carole Lombard, died in an air crash in 1942 while returning from a War Bond drive, he left MGM and joined the Army，或 Clark Gable left MGM and joined the Army when his wife, Carole Lombard, died in an air crash in 1942 while returning from a War Bond drive.

看標語學英文

臺灣高鐵廣播，Please conduct your conversation with a low tone of voice. 句字不順，又囉唆，直接寫：Please speak softly.

也可以說 Please don't shout. 或 Lower your voice when you talk.

又：with a low tone of voice 不對，英文是 in a low tone of voice
但不如寫漂亮的句子。

Practice Writing

Complete these sentences. Give your imagination free play. If possible, write a whole story for each. Use no unnecessary words.

She stared in disbelief as her computer ____________________

For the last five generations, their family struggled ________________

During her ten years on the police force, she had __________________

Potato chips are ____________________

The sapling was free, so ____________________

Write a sentence for each of these words.

- prevail
- bound
- file
- morale
- stem

Write an essay.

Write about your experience with the novel coronavirus, COVID-19.

甚麼叫做「日耳曼」、「拉丁」字？

現在的英國，最早居民說 Celtic 凱爾特語言，現在的威爾斯語、蘇格蘭語、愛爾蘭語就是。Celtic 屬于印歐語系，與日耳曼為表兄弟加鄰居，與拉丁文為很遠的表兄妹，與希臘語同宗，但更遠。

Celtic 族過著自己的日子，無奈好戰的維京來侵略，跟著來很多其它日耳曼族來霸佔 Celtic 的地盤；這些侵略者操的日耳曼語，類似現在的德語、英語。Celtic 語慢慢退，被 Anglo-Saxon 的日耳曼語取代。

另一族北方人，諾曼 Normans（north men，北人）霸佔了法國北邊，吸收法國文化、語言。法國情形類似不列顛，他們本來也操 Celtic，但被羅馬的拉丁文取代。羅馬帝國解體，屬地各自為政，交通不便，他們講的拉丁文慢慢演變成地方語言：義大利語、法語、西班牙語等。所以住法國的北人說的是法國化的拉丁語。與日耳曼同為印歐語系，但屬旁系；有人誤以為英語屬于拉丁語宗，或從拉丁文演變而來：錯。

Anglo-Saxons 在不列顛過著自己的日子，北人的君王 King William 想吃掉他們的土地，一〇六六年越過英國海峽侵略不列顛；主場的 King Harold 帶隊來 Hastings 迎戰。

歷史樞紐在一矢。鏖戰時，北人流矢射中 King Harold 眼睛，他率領的弟兄們潰不成軍，北人獲勝，他們的君王升級為 William the Conqueror。他統治不列顛，規定所有政府相關單位要講法語，因此帶了非常多拉丁系的字到英文。不知道哪位北人軍的弟兄幹的好事。如果風吹一下，那支矢偏左偏右，也許我們現在講的英語全然不同。但事實如此，所以英語成了大雜燴。

Chapter 19 字彙運用：同義詞未必都通用

Words, Words, and More Words

孔子說，必也正名乎！名不正則言不順；言不順則事不成；事不成則禮樂不興；禮樂不興則刑罰不中；刑罰不中則民無所措手足。故君子明之必可言也，言之必可行也。君子于其言，無所苟而已矣。孔子講的話，都很有道理。為甚麼要正名呢？因為如果我們隨意亂用字，無法溝通。

隨意亂用字，一則無法溝通，一則自己理路不清。在此不必細論，但人腦的思索，大多以語言運轉，所以如果沒弄清楚字意，概念模糊，思維很難清晰。尤其讀書人靠三寸不爛之舌生存，該明白字意，不該人云亦云、不假思索將流行字眼掛在嘴上。

寫作該發揮字彙：豐富字彙優美，又精簡。閱讀可快可慢，讀者可以思索、停頓、重讀，所以寫作句型、詞彙比口說深。

英文字彙有一點點像中文的成語：成語用得好，言簡意賅；如果知道的很少，給人的感覺是沒受過教育。但用太多，很炫耀，讓人厭倦。

Don't use a word just because you have heard others use it. 有些常見字，時下用法已偏離正意。

用詞先決條件是要明白字詞正確意思；學字彙不宜盲從追隨，別人說我就盲目用詞；要了解字義、含義、用法。來介紹幾個字彙。

Significant，有意義，由 sign 得義，指出。Significant 的意思是「有意義」：Their dog's name is Rover，句子通，字用對，意義清楚，這就是 significant。Today is Monday：此句語意清楚、文法通，就是 significant。若寫火星語，The yellow Monday whispered through the mysterious potato，不知所云，這就是 not significant，就這麼簡單。他們的狗叫什麼名字、星期幾，影響大局嗎？很重要嗎？句子 significant，但未必重要。重要就 important 啦，不要將 significant 當 important 的代替詞。

> 用詞謹慎的人不把 significant 當作「重要」：
> 可用 important、momentous、influential、extraordinary、prominent。

While 應該是很簡單的字：同時。Marvin figured out the numbers in his head while he was waiting for the bus. 當他等公車時，他同時用心算算數字。簡單吧，要用錯，需要一點天賦。

While Custer's men tried to ford the river, Cheyenne and Sioux sharpshooters fired at them continuously. 美國歷史上鼎鼎大名的 Battle of the Greasy Grass（亦名 the Battle of the Little Big Horn 或 Custer's Last Stand）發生在一八七六年六月廿六日，宇宙間只有那天那個時間才發生了這些事，while 字需要講得這麼詳細嗎？需要，因為竟然有人會用錯！

While 也有「然而」的用法，但無論如何用，必須含「同時」的意思。
Andrea thought that there was no need to continue, while Adam still thought they could make their relationship succeed.

在我們的宇宙，while,「同時」，發生在同一個時間點上。Henry lived in Hsinchu until he was sixteen while he moved to Taipei the following year. 這怎麼可能呢？

Major 是 minor 的反義詞。醫學用法恰當：major surgery 關係生命，minor surgery，如骨折裝釘，正常情況下不會死人。Major 不要當 big

的替用詞，要大就 big, large, huge, gigantic, immense, tremendous, massive, vast，只要注意各字的含意，任君選。

Enormous 正確意思是負面的。

Impact 正確意思是撞擊，名詞，例如醉翁撞牆，碰！頭破了洞，這是 impact。文筆好的人不當 influence 的同義詞。Influence 可抽象可具體，impact 最好還是留著「撞擊」的意思。更不該當動詞用。

Passion 也是濫用字。Passion 字根為痛苦、忍痛。痛，忍一忍就過了；本來的意思是逆來順受、忍受、受苦。英文早期用法，專指耶穌釘在十字架的苦難：極難忍，一個下午就過了。後來指疾病，再往後當作無法駕馭的強烈情緒，喜怒哀樂失控，而後陡然消失，就是 passion。再後來，又當作慾望、慾火焚身，但發作一回就過了。廿一世紀初，申請學校的讀書計畫都要寫 I have a passion for biology or electrical engineering or interior design. 💣 陳腔濫調千篇一律，很煩，很空洞，執筆彷彿想強調用詞不謹慎、沒創意。改為 enthusiasm、fascination、zeal，但猶不如敘述狀況。

字首 **de**、**dis** 表示下、棄、否定。Interest 本意為「利益」，引伸為「好奇、注意的心態」，有兩種否定：uninterested 是「不感興趣」，disinterested 是「沒有利害關係、超然、客觀」，兩者必辨。法官需要 disinterested 且不可 uninterested。

華語背景人將 interesting 當作「有趣、有意思」，所以用此字，偏離英語用法。

Intellectual，形容詞名詞兼用，由 intellect、intelligent 而生。Intellect，判辨能力、知識、推理能力；intelligent，聰明，耳聰目明。此二字迥異于 wisdom：智慧。Wisdom 的字根 *weid，意思是「看」：

wisdom 的基本要素，看很多、想很多、看很透。Intellect、intelligent 字根 *leg，字、言、說、教；我家的狗很聰明，可是沒有智慧。很不幸，臺灣律師英文程度不夠，誤將 intellectual 譯為「智慧」，所以有「智慧財產權」，因而產生「智慧型手機」等等錯誤概念。對岸律師英文比較好，譯為「智能」，才對。

Literally，字根與 letter、literature 有關，「依照字面解釋的」，是 figuratively，「比喻」的反義詞。如果中午沒時間吃便當，到下午很餓，說，I am starving，這是figurative，比喻，因為說實話，再撐一下，頂多減肥；如乞丐討不到飯，幾天沒吃，有生命危險，說，I am starving，這是 literal。不要隨意用來加強語氣：I literally died laughing：安息吧，何時火化？

時下流行 **unique**。字根與 one 有關。Unique，獨一無二。是絕對的，只有一個，所以不能修飾。現在很多英美人士說 very unique, extremely unique 之類的無腦詞，翻中文就知道問題：非常獨一無二、極端獨一無二：難道也可以說「稍微獨一無二」嗎？Unique 就是 unique，無從比較無法調整語氣：Every person's DNA is unique。字彙資源豐厚的人寫 extraordinary, special, exceptional, memorable, distinguished, distinctive。

Effective，有效、導致預期的效果，形容詞：Masks proved effective at stopping the spread of COVID-19. 缺乏基本文學素養的官僚喜歡當副詞，自從：The price will be raised effective next Monday. 此句刪 effective，或換 beginning。

多多練英語，加強字彙，明白字義，下筆撰寫更順。

Improve these sentences.

1. Nobody really knows if this is true or not, and nobody knows who said it first, but on the internet people are playing games, and some of them are saying that on this one game, it's a game called Dead Bread, people say that there are characters who can walk around, but they're actually dead people who have come back to life and they are really dangerous and hard to deal with.

2. Amber was so shocked that she couldn't believe it was real when Kyle told her something he didn't want anybody else to know.

3. There's a place where the workers put things together, it's like a long line and everybody has a particular job to do, and the things they are making keep going at the same speed, without getting faster or slower.

4. There were a lot of people there and he walked very carefully but as he was going along, some person bumped into him and almost made him lose his footing and later he suddenly found out that that person had taken his wallet.

5. Nothing really important happened, but Donald was really irritated and couldn't control himself so he was in a bad temper and made sure everybody knew it.

參考例句

❶ An internet rumor claims that there are zombies in the online game, Dead Bread.
rumor, gossip, tattle (v)

❷ Amber was incredulous when Kyle revealed a secret.
incredulous, astonished, skeptical, dumbfounded

❸ On the assembly line, the products move forward at a uniform speed.
uniform, orderly, fixed, consistent

❹ He realized he had been jostled by a pickpocket as he wended his way through the crowd.
jostle, bump into

❺ Donald was petulant.
petulant, sulking, brooding, sour, fretful, grumpy, irritable, morose, pouting

Practice Writing

Complete these sentences. Use your imagination. Don't be trite, don't be lazy.

The difference between a cellphone and a camera is ________

The little boy reached into his pocket for ________________

The old lady reached into her pocket for ________________

They hadn't expected the water level in the river to be so high ________________

A bit of chocolate ________________

Write a sentence for each of these words.

- splice
- whistle
- partial
- tolerable
- liable

Write an essay.

What are you good at? It might be geography, or baking cakes, or getting along with cats, or playing the kashaka. Write about what you are good at. How did you get interested in this?

Be specific, give details.

Chapter 20 挑字邏輯：適當性優先
The Logic of Words

撰文目的是傳達訊息？或爬滿格子賺稿費？要傳達訊息，先問自己想好了要傳達的意義嗎？讀者目的是吸收訊息？或僅僅求娛樂、消磨時間？

如果沒傳達清楚，想吸收訊息的讀者會分心。邏輯緊湊，是文章的經緯，作品越長越見功夫；邏輯疏散的人寫不出好文章（意識流小說除外）。

毒梟販毒，兩方一言不合就火拼，美國新聞報導常寫 the drug deal went wrong。請問，甚麼樣的販毒算 go right ？一手交錢一手交貨，兩方逍遙法外就是 right ？人云亦云、不思索，往往是這種下場。

英文可看到這類句子：He was a former Marine.
從前是陸戰隊的，但動詞用過去式；他回到部隊了嗎？寫 He is a former Marine 就很清楚。乾脆寫 He was a Marine.

時常看到 center around：The classic comedy, The Blues Brothers, centers around the misadventures of two jazz musicians trying to pay a debt. 眾所周知，center 是中央、中心、核心；around 是周圍、圍繞。怎麼可能又是中心又在附近圍繞？正確的用法是 center on。

崛起，許多文章寫 meteoric rise。Meteor，隕石；rise，升起。隕，說文解字：從高下也。下且升，這樣對得起地心引力嗎？

時下用 quantum leap 來形容突飛猛進，聽起來很炫。此詞流行，也許起因於一九九〇年代的電視劇，加上對物理學的景仰、一知半解。但想一想，肉眼看不到量子，它「躍遷」能跳多遠？物理學者認為量子「躍遷」好比雪融，不快，所以用 quantum leap 描述突飛猛進，怎樣不合理。

Head over heels 形容翻跟斗，尤指熱戀中的情人（尤其男性），愛的神昏顛倒。但正常情形，人的頭當然高于腳跟。

Veneer 是「單板」，用來裝飾三夾板的薄片木材；文中當作浮淺表層、虛假的表面。Veneer 通常厚度不到 3mm，所以文中 thin veneer，thin 字冗，刪。

Underpinning 是地基，地下支撐或強化建築。引伸為基本理論，所以 basic underpinning，邏輯疏劣。

> A designer knows he has achieved perfection not when there is nothing left to add, but when there is nothing left to take away.
>
> 法國作家／ Antoine de Saint-Exupery

Lesson IV
道地英文寫作訣竅

Chapter 21 訣竅一：擺脫死水架構

撰文，要表達清楚，但不要把讀者當笨蛋，不必太清楚；換言之，寫清楚，但毋需寫太清楚。

👎 在她當總經理的任期內的時間裡
爬格子嗎？
她當總經理的任期內
已經很清楚。寫「她當總經理時」有何不好？

👎 橡皮擦掉下去到桌下地板上。
桌下，如果不掉在地板，請問到哪去了？除非強調沒掉到垃圾桶，不必寫地板。此句二「下」，掉難道掉到天花板？橡皮擦掉到桌下。

律師寫作有他們的考量，可是誰無聊時拿起契約來閱讀？看過扣人心弦的狀子嗎？我們撰文不要效法律師。我們寫清楚，恰到好處：不要寫太多，不要寫太少。

解釋太清楚，就是藐視讀者：He tore the paper in half, so as a result he had two pieces of paper。難道撕半就會有六張嗎？

She drank a cup of hot coffee that had been made from coffee beans and was served steaming hot.
正常情況下，咖啡是用咖啡豆泡的。除非強調不是即溶咖啡，不必寫豆。熱咖啡本來就熱，不必重述。
She drank a cup of steaming hot coffee.

閱讀是思考：如果剝奪讀者自己想的機會，就沒興趣往下讀。除非寫使用說明，提示就夠了；讀者自己思索，才能投入文字。

Smoking cigarettes on a regular basis, frequently without consciously making a decision to smoke a cigarette, tends to be an indication of a problem related to addictive behavior.

改：**Smoking habitually is a sign of addiction.**

We plan to attend the showing of a moving picture and will be accompanied by our friend Huang who has just arrived on a visit from the southern city of Kaohsiung.

改：**We will go to a movie with Huang, who is visiting from Kaohsiung.**

評：如果讀者可能不知道「高雄」在哪，考慮保留 the southern city。

In the early beginnings of his career, Lin had an uphill climb and applied himself to his work assiduously to attain a better situation.

評：此句可真不知該如何救。Beginning 顧名思義，當然是 early。Climb 本是 uphill。apply yourself、assiduously、attain a better situation，這種十八世紀的英文已發霉。除非是富二代，剛出道的人 要往上爬當然要努力。還需要說明嗎？看全文的方向。如果要保留，寫 Early in his career, Lin struggled to get ahead，尚可。沒有更好的內容可以寫嗎？假若此 struggle 重要，寫具體：他如何發憤圖強？ 他遇到何種障礙？光說 struggle，空洞，引不起讀者興趣。

Practice Writing

Complete these sentences. Think a bit. Be sure to write something vivid.

As we sat on the beach ____________________

You are free to ____________________

At the end of the ____________________

When the police opened the shoebox, they discovered ____________________

The riderless horse ____________________

Write a sentence for each of these words.

- restore
- offensive
- reconciliation
- budding
- compass

Write an essay.

We all make mistakes. Write about a big mistake you made, or an especially embarrassing mistake, or a mistake that taught you something important.

Chapter 22 訣竅二：神助攻的私房書單

文書的基本要求是傳達意旨。小朋友寫「小恩是大笨蛋」，也算寫作。但讀書人下筆，應當不只如此。

首先，讀書人該注意字義。字義不明，與他人無法溝通，內在思路不清楚。還有呢，讀書人，談吐、下筆，多少應該有點文學氣息。這需要培養。中文，可以從《古文觀止》讀起。先看歐陽修的文章，宋明讀完，從唐末倒著讀到魏晉南北朝，再來漢朝，最後讀周秦文。或者隨便甚麼順序，可以隨意翻開讀，也可以讓貓幫你選，但須慢慢讀，仔細看古人怎麼寫。

英文，先不看古英文。推薦幾本書，沒甚麼順序：
James Joyce, *A Portrait of the Artist as a Young Man*
E M Forster, *A Passage to India*
J J Tolkien, *The Lord of the Rings*
Ursula Leguin, *A Wizard of Earthsea*
Margaret Atwood*, The Handmaid's Tale*
Frank Herbert, *Dune*
Norton Juster, *The Phantom Tollbooth*
Harper Lee, *To Kill a Mockingbird*
John Steinbeck, *The Grapes of Wrath*
Jared Diamond, Guns, *Germs, and Steel*

一篇好的文學作品或藝術品，
看過後五年再看，
如果感覺與第一次看一樣，
恭喜，白活五年了。

好書很多，此單子起頭而已。上列的書，都容易看，文字不深。書單沒有外文作品，因為各家翻譯優劣不一。若要接受挑戰，讀 Joseph Conrad 的作品，如 *The Heart of Darkness* 或 *Lord Jim*。他的作品探索人生，故事生動，但文筆程度較高，字彙豐富，句型結構複雜，比較難懂。不要氣餒：這位波蘭作家十幾歲才學英文，二十幾歲才算流俐。

現在美國高中生多讀 *The Great Gatsby*，本猩認為只是敘述富豪，所以有人垂涎，而故事、文筆平平。本猩列書單，當然主觀，若不服，歡迎自己開單子，多多益善。

反正，多讀就是了。多讀，慢慢就知道字的含意、程度、層面、韻味，也習慣英文表達法。

很多期刊可以讀。本猩認為目前文筆、廣度、深度最好的期刊是 *The Atlantic Monthly*。*The New Yorker*、*Harper's Magazine* 也不乏好文章。重點是讀者有興趣看，會繼續讀、用心讀、雞蛋裏挑骨頭地讀。

建議下載 Pocket app。下載時勾選興趣，app 會傳相關文章，大體文筆不錯。每篇注明閱讀時間需要幾分鍾，可以有心理準備。

> 甚善、極佳、很讚：意思相近；寫 Line 給朋友，會寫甚善嗎？寫年終考績，寫「很讚」合適嗎？
>
> 一字一詞，屬于常用、冷僻、高雅、低俗，要怎麼判辨？靠經驗。多讀英美文章，慢慢了解。

我們來分析一篇千古不朽的好文章。本是演講稿，卻屬上好文學作品看：鼎鼎大名的 Gettysburg Address。

先講背景。美國南北戰爭（一八六一至一八六五年），擁護黑奴制度的南軍在一八六三年打到賓州的 Gettysburg，三天劇戰，南軍敗績，而兩敗俱傷：叛軍陣亡兩萬七千人，北軍兩萬三千英雄殉國。政府就地建立墓園，一八六三年十一月十九日開幕典禮，林肯總統致詞。

請讀者念出聲音：
Four score and seven years ago, our fathers brought forth on this continent, a new nation, conceived in liberty, and dedicated to the proposition that all men are created equal.

Now we are engaged in a great civil war, testing whether that nation, or any nation so conceived and so dedicated, can long endure. We are met on a great battlefield of that war. We have come to dedicate a portion of that field, as a final resting place for those who here gave their lives that that nation might live. It is altogether fitting and proper that we should do this.

But, in a larger sense, we can not dedicate — we can not consecrate — we can not hallow — this ground. The brave men, living and dead, who struggled here, have consecrated it, far above our poor power to add or detract. The world will little note, nor long remember what we say here, but it can never forget what they did here. It is for us the living, rather, to be dedicated here to the unfinished work which they who fought here have thus far so nobly advanced. It is rather for us to be here dedicated to the great task remaining before us — that from these honored dead we take increased devotion to that cause for which they gave the last full measure of devotion — that we here highly resolve that these dead shall not have died in vain — that this nation, under God, shall have a new birth of freedom — and that government of the people, by the people, for the people, shall not perish from the earth.

請再念一次，這次跟著輕重音、句法拍節奏。

可聽到前段多音節的字，如 conceived、dedicated、proposition，用比較多，後段很多單音節字：these dead shall not have died in vain。你認為這是為甚麼？從頭讀。

廿為一 score。美國一七七六年宣布獨立，離林肯演講八十七年；本猩一再強調刪贅字，為甚麼反而讚許總統用的這個古怪算法？請念念看：

In 1776, our fathers brought forth a new nation.
87 years ago, our fathers brought forth a new nation.
Four score and seven years ago, our fathers brought forth a new nation.

林肯總統顧慮節奏；突然報出一七七六、八十七，險峻；說 four score and seven years，序曲拉長，讓人思考時間。另一個問題，in、eight 是母音，嘴巴開，four 的 f 是單唇音，容易起音。林肯文學素養、演講經驗夠，念一念就選此開場白。

聖經說人生大限 three score years and ten，特別強壯的人可以活 four score years，林肯這句也提醒生死大。但那是林肯總統，我們不可以用這種算法，以免笑話。

第一句用古老怪語，立即講到美國嶄新國家、嶄新理念。接著，提醒聽眾，我們的前輩建國理念：人人平等，言外之意是，怎可容許奴隸制度？請注意，林肯從一七七六獨立宣言講起，而不從一七八七立憲講，因為美國人盡知，獨立宣言第一句說 all men are created equal，而憲法默許奴隸制。

南方堅持奴隸制度，導致內戰。美國建國，是歷史上首一民主共和國，稱為 great experiment；歐洲貴族認為不可能持久，絕不能 long endure，等著看笑話；這場戰是考驗，許多英雄為國捐軀，我們為他們建立墓園，這是應該的。

[They] brought forth a new nation, conceived in liberty；gave their lives that that nation might live；the brave men, living and dead；it is for us, the living；shall have a new birth of freedom：生與死、死與生，對比極強烈。

演講第一字是 Four， 此段 battlefield、field、final、for、lives、live、fitting，一串 f/v 音，回音也回應。

林肯曾當律師、議員，法律根基深厚，所以講 fitting and proper，類似英語法律常用疊詞，fitting 是日耳曼字根，proper 是拉丁字根。

才剛說我們應該這樣紀念他們，馬上反過來說我們不能，用三句（請念出）：we can not dedicate — we can not consecrate — we can not hallow — this ground。又，dedicate、consecrate 是拉丁字根， 最後重點落在 hallow，日耳曼字，語源近英語：由遠而近。

又：現在寫法，cannot 當一字，而在茲寫兩個字，一則十九世紀的用法，一則加強語氣，分開念。

The brave men 一句，既禮敬戰士，又強調，我們只說話，他們真的做到了。說 living and dead，生與死。

The world will little note, nor long remember what we say here, but it can never forget what they did here，很漂亮的對句。範圍現在從美國擴展到全世界，以示敬意。

Unfinished work，演講時叛國賊尚未歸順。第一句在八十七年前，今天舉行儀式，未來我們還有工作。注意 living 與 dead、not have died 與 a new birth 的對照，生與死。

許多崇高理想字眼：dedicated、nobly、great、honored、devotion、highly resolve、god、birth、freedom。

死了，若簡單說 died，在此無力，gave the last full measure of devotion，呼應 dedication。

Of the people, by the people, for the people，三句，十字闡明美國民主精神（又啟發孫中山先生的三民主義）。

內戰期國家岌岌可危，所以說 shall not perish，而不說 will live forever。

英文泛指人通常用 you，we 比中文的「我們」範圍小，你同我，你們同我們；三百字不到，講 we 十次。講八次 here，dedicate 講了六次，一再將聽眾拉到現場的儀式。國家分裂，所以 nation 提了五次。

英文與拉丁文是表兄妹，與德文是堂兄弟，所以對 native speaker 來說，雖然可能未曾意識到，而日耳曼字比較親近、說服力強。英語的日耳曼字短、勁，拉丁字長，自然散、弱。開頭很多拉丁字：nation 而不是 country，liberty 而不是 freedom，比較正式，法律意味濃。權威而不親，所以後文多日耳曼字：these dead shall not have died in vain—that this nation, under God, shall have a new birth of freedom.

深厚文學根基滋養字句。Four score and seven years ago 取自 KJV Bible 的寫法；例如，《創世紀》說 Abraham 生兒子時，fourscore and six years old。他沒說民主可能消失，卻取材于約伯：his branch shall be cut off; his remembrance shall perish from the earth.

林肯小時勤讀修辭，課本的對比法、平行句、語音協調習題很難。他愛朗讀，很喜歡朗誦詩給朋友聽，並細讀 Bacon 的散文、the King James Bible（KJV，宗教文學，中古英文文筆的極致）、Shakespeare：*Hamlet, King Lear, Macbeth, Richard III, Henry VIII* 讀過幾十遍。

這篇偉大，也是因為林肯沒有刻意運用各種技巧，他憑一生的閱讀、寫作、人生歷練，結合總統的考驗、同胞的憐憫、愛國的決心，寫出這篇。這不是一般人能寫的。

或許有人問，文筆那麼重要嗎？表達意思就好了，管它文筆好不好。

不容易看懂，若歸咎于讀者程度不夠，不是作者的問題。倘若寫作草率，讀者要讀第二遍才明白，很容易分心。寫作要傳達訊息，如果讀者讀不下去，白寫了。

抓住讀者興趣，並非易事，不要讓讀者分心。

陳阿貓與林阿狗當過總經理，前者在民國九十三年離職，後者在民國九十九年離職。

讀者需要停下，整理一下：前者是陳阿貓，後者是林阿狗，所以陳總九十三年離職，林董九十九年離職。這樣停下、回頭對照，讀者分心了，文章效果銳減。

陳阿貓總經理在民國九十三年辭職，林阿狗總經理在民國九十九年退休。

句子容易懂，且比較具體。

更甚者，我看過這類句子：

Irene and Grace both graduated from Kansas State in 1942, the latter studying Literature and the former studying Library Management.

不要鬧了！ 盡量少用 respective 或 respectively；句子結構好，不必用。

讀者整理句子，分心了，文章效果弱了。

Irene and Grace studied Library Management and Literature respectively.

不能寫好一點嗎？
Irene studied Library Management, and Grace studied Literature.
Irene studied Library Management, and Grace, Literature.
Irene studied Library Management; Grace, Literature.

Management 後的逗點還是要，以免讀者看成 Irene studied Library Management and Grace：Irene 工讀圖書管理、餐前禱告。

從英文名判斷你的出生年代

英文名字有時代特質。Irene 在一九一〇年代流行過，再來幾乎只有華人取這個名字。Grace 從一八八〇年代退流行後，幾乎消失，二十一世紀登場復活了一段時日，又退下去了。

本書例句的人名，以美國社會為準，適合現在（西元二〇二二年）二十歲到四十歲的人，除非上文 Irene and Grace 之類，標明是很久以前的人。所以本書中不見 Fred, Betty, Arthur, Linda, Frank, Alice, Agnes, Richard, Mary 等老人家的名字。Karen 是奧客代表。

Chapter 23 訣竅三：集合相關字

一篇文章寫出去，如果讀者程度不夠，看不懂句子，他家的事；但如果寫的不夠好，讀者必須回頭整理才看懂，這是作者沒有盡職；好比菜上桌時沒煮熟，客人還要料理才能吃。文章給他人看，寫者要先負責字句通順，不該要求讀者整理、修補、編寫才看懂。

所謂「通順」，字句通、章法順。如若句不通、章不順、讀者不容易看懂，表示寫的人沒寫好。讀者沒有義務為作者編輯文章。如果讀者要整理文句才看懂，分心了，文章效果銳減。

相關字詞排在一起，以免讀者困惑。

Bethany was the only woman in the group of friends wearing red.
「在一群穿紅衣的朋友，Bethany 是唯一的女性。」是這個意思嗎？到底有幾位女士？誰穿紅色？ Bethany 或 the group of friends? 似乎是 the group of friends，但又可能是 Bethany。

如果是，就要寫清楚：
Bethany was the only woman wearing red in the group of friends.

也可能排列：
Bethany, wearing red, was the only woman in the group of friends.
Wearing red, Bethany was the only woman in the group of friends.
可通，而不順，且不知道為何強調她穿紅衣。

The patient was struck by the brick in her nose.
第一眼看，以爲鼻裏藏磚。
改為：The patient was struck in the nose by the brick.
還是不漂亮。換：
The brick struck the patient in the nose.

主詞與主動辭間不排片語，片語調句首。
The birds sitting on the branches sang.
Sitting on the branches, the birds sang.

再舉例：
The investigators discovered weeks ago the terrorist bought materials to make a bomb.
非常 ambiguous：到底是幾週前發現的呢？或恐怖份子幾週前買了材料？加了 that 就明瞭。

The investigators discovered weeks ago that the terrorist bought materials to make a bomb.
The investigators discovered that weeks ago the terrorist bought materials to make a bomb.

若是前幾週發現的，也可以寫：
Weeks ago, the investigators discovered the terrorist bought materials to make a bomb.
The investigators discovered, weeks ago the terrorist bought materials to make a bomb.

不寫 that 而加逗點，句子有點弱。若寫
The investigators discovered the terrorist bought materials to make a bomb weeks ago.
似乎炸彈是前幾週製造的。

寫作本來就不容易，需要多修改、重寫。基本條件是，需要熟悉英文句型、字彙。

英文還有一種叫做 **garden path sentences** 引入歧途句：讀者很容易斷錯句。

I told her children are supposed to be mischievous.
讀者很容易認為，I told her children，我告訴她的小孩，下半句就接不上。
本意是，我告訴了她，小孩子調皮才對。怎麼救呢？易爾：加 that。

I told her that children are supposed to be mischievous.

嬰孩當然吃食物，不是嗎？
When babies eat food gets wasted.
注意標點。
When babies eat, food gets wasted.

The doctor told us she will be here for the party yesterday.
寫作不慎，似乎時態不協；只要 yesterday 移位便明白了：
Yesterday the doctor told us she will be here for the party.
The doctor told us yesterday she will be here for the party.

Have the students who finished their tests already doublecheck their answers.
Have 起頭的句子往往是現在完成式問句。讀者預期這類句：Have the students who finished their tests already doublechecked their answers? 而沒有過去分詞、問號，反而句點收句，怎麼解讀？原來寫作草率，句型是：have N V 吩咐。太容易誤會，所以改寫：Tell the students who finished their tests already to doublecheck their answers.

（說話時，因爲有語調、節奏，原來字句沒問題。）

Garden path sentence 的由來

為何叫 garden path sentence ？起自 lead someone down (up) the garden path 一語。花園小徑多彎曲，甚至不通，所以引人走園徑，帶入死胡同、騙人、耍手段。

在網路發現 garden path sentence 妙句：
I ate a kid's meal at Mickey D's today.
His mom was really upset.

My wife complained to me that I never buy her flowers.
To be honest, I really never had a clue she was selling flowers.

Improve these sentences

❶ Sarah joined the concert by the Philharmonic Orchestra with her friend Marissa.

❷ The hostess served blonde roast coffee to the guests in exquisite porcelain cups.

❸ The scientists studied the fossils of extinct dinosaurs which are dead in Arizona.

❹ Allison almost worked in the office wearing green pants at that point in time.

❺ The parents wanted to find a tutor for their daughter who didn't smoke or drink.

難嗎？學英文，就是要多背單字，多練習！

參考例句

❶ **Sarah went with her friend Marissa to the Philharmonic Orchestra concert.**

評：華語背景的人將 join 與「參加」畫上等號：join 是成為團員、會員的程序，若譯「辦理入會手續」，比較接近英語用法。
若不嫌逗點太多，亦可寫 Sarah went with her friend, Marissa, to the Philharmonic Orchestra concert. 亦可寫 Sarah went with Marissa, her friend, to the Philharmonic Orchestra concert. 稍嫌不順。

❷ **The hostess served the guests blonde roast coffee in exquisite porcelain cups.**

評：依原句，客人坐在瓷杯裏。如果不需要強調 hostess，可寫 Blonde roast coffee in exquisite porcelain cups was served to the guests. The guests were served blonde roast coffee in exquisite porcelain cups.

❸ **In Arizona, the scientists studied the fossils of extinct dinosaurs.**
In Arizona, the scientists studied the dinosaur fossils.

評：Extinct 的定義就是 dead，不必贅敘；恐龍已絕種，眾所周知，extinct 也可以刪。但無論如何，死掉了，到哪裏都是死的，若寫 dead in Arizona，難道到了加州就復活？

❹ **Allison almost always wore green pants to work then.**

評：Allison almost worked，表示她實際上沒有工作； almost 的意思是「幾乎、差一點」，很多學員當作 almost always「幾乎每次」用。At that point in time，囉唆：then。需不需要說明 in the office，可斟酌。

❺ **The parents wanted to find a tutor who didn't smoke or drink for their daughter.**

評：當然，可能雙親有一位抽菸喝酒的女兒，一位不抽菸不喝酒的女兒，要幫不抽菸不喝酒的女兒找家教老師，菸酒女兒自己想辦法；若是，原句不改。

輕鬆一下

網路上，某甲問：

Can you shoot a squirrel with a .22 rifle from a mile away?

某乙回：

This is a ridiculous question. Squirrels do not have .22 rifles. However, if one did, I certainly could shoot it from one mile away with a sniper rifle. That would teach the squirrel he should not carry a .22 rifle.

Combine these sentences.

❶ Maurice Herzog was a climber. He was from France. With a team of mountaineers, Herzog climbed a mountain called Annapurna. Annapurna is a mountain which is over 8,000 meters high. This was the first time anybody had climbed a mountain that was 8,000 meters or more. They summited on June 3, 1950.

❷ There is a small celestial body. It is about the size of a car. It was captured by the earth's orbit in 2017. It is considered to be the earth's second moon.

新月球定名 2020 CD3a。嫦娥現在有別墅了。

❸ Tahini is a paste. Making it is a tradition in the Mideast. They hull sesame seeds to make it. Tahini is rich in protein. It is very, very good if you need energy. People use tahini and then use chickpeas, and they make hummus. Hummus is a dish that tastes very good and has a very good flavor.

❹ The School of Dentistry at New York University conducted a study. They studied vaping. The study shows something that happens to people who vape. The composition of the bacteria in their mouth actually changes. Because of this, it is easier for them to get infections and inflammations in their mouth.

❺ **Datunshan is a mountain located on the northwest part of the Taipei Basin. The elevation of the mountain is 1092 meters. It is a live volcano. Scientists discovered that it is a live volcano in 2016. A lot of people live in the Taipei Basin. People live very close together in the Taipei Basin. Geologists say the volcano will erupt some day, but it will not erupt very soon.**

Datunshan，大屯山

❻ **Colorado was admitted to the Union in 1876. Five months before that, people there founded the University of Colorado in Boulder. The university opened the next year. There were fifteen students. In 1878, the university hired its first female professor. Her name was Mary Rippon.**

寫作小叮嚀

一般華人寫英文，落于兩個極端：句子都很短，否則全串在一起，全文僅一超長句，主詞早已不見蹤影，找不到句點。寫者該求中庸之道，長短句相參。

但因為一般學生不太能寫正確長句，所以本書提供很多練習。並不表示撰文都要用長句。長短相參。

參考例句

❶ **On June 3, 1950, the French climber Maurice Herzog and his team became the first climbers to reach the summit of an 8,000 meter peak, Annapurna.**

❷ **A small celestial body about the size of a car was captured by the earth's orbit in 2017, and is considered to be the earth's second moon, as it fits the astronomical definition of a moon.**

❸ **Tahini, a traditional Mideastern paste made from hulled sesame seeds, is rich in protein, an excellent energy source, and combined with chickpeas to make the savory dish, hummus.**

評：一句不要裝太多內容。考慮分兩句。Tahini, a traditional Mideastern paste made from hulled sesame seeds, is rich in protein, and is an excellent energy source. It is combined with chickpeas to make the savory dish, hummus.
為何用 savory，不寫 delicious ？前文不可避免 sesame seeds，四個 s 音，若在此寫 delicious dish，嫌重音太多，不悅耳（二 d，又 cious、sh）。見仁見智。

❹ **A study conducted by the School of Dentistry at New York University shows that vaping actually changes the bacterial composition in the smoker's mouth, leaving them more susceptible to infection and inflammation.**

❺ **In 2016, geologists discovered that Datunshan, a 1092 meter mountain on the northwest rim of the densely populated Taipei Basin, is a live volcano, but is not likely to erupt soon.**

評：Is not likely to erupt soon 的 is 可省；依作者想要的節奏而取捨。

❻ **The University of Colorado Boulder was founded five months before Colorado was admitted to the Union in 1876, opened in 1877 with fifteen students, and hired its first female professor, Mary Rippon, in 1878.**
The University of Colorado Boulder was founded in 1876, five months before Colorado was admitted to the Union, opened in 1877 with fifteen students, and in 1878 hired its first female professor, Mary Rippon.

輕鬆一下

The law says you have to turn on your headlights when it's raining in Sweden.

How am I supposed to know when it's raining in Sweden?

Practice writing

Complete these sentences. Use your imagination.

She saw the hornet ______________________________

As the firefighters fought the blaze, they discovered __________

As punishment for insubordination, the soldier __________

Six lightyears from Earth ____________________

The police needed to simplify __________

Write a sentence for each of these words.

- manners
- film
- taciturn
- superfluous
- stake

Write an essay.

Write about something frustrating that happened to you. Explain what led to it, why it frustrated you, and how you dealt with it. Give details, tell a story.

Chapter 24 訣竅四：第一句就要抓眼球

開場第一句最重要。如果首句沒抓住讀者興趣，誰看下文？

英國作家 Charles Dickens (1812 – 1870), *A Tale of Two Cities* 頭一句響亮：

It was the best of times, it was the worst of times, it was the age of wisdom, it was the age of foolishness, it was the epoch of belief, it was the epoch of incredulity, it was the season of Light, it was the season of Darkness, it was the spring of hope, it was the winter of despair, we had everything before us, we had nothing before us, we were all going direct to Heaven, we were all going direct the other way – in short, the period was so far like the present period, that some of its noisiest authorities insisted on its being received, for good or for evil, in the superlative degree of comparison only.

這是大師的文筆。一般作者很難寫出那麼長、又不疏散的句子。

不只第一句要響亮，頭一字不該太虛，除非能夠像 Dickens 此句由柔漸剛、如漲潮登涯。簡單說，頭一字盡量不要寫 it。除非你能寫出 *A Tale of Two Cities* 。

請想下列情景，寫開場第一句，要響亮，引人入勝，但不可落入俗套。不要太快下筆。這砲怎麼開？從哪個角度寫？想像、斟酌、選字。
A young woman is entering the army. This is her first day.

Hoeing his field, the farmer found a pistol.

Two ducks are paddling in shallow water.

A woman answers the phone. The police tell her that her daughter has been arrested for murder.

A young man has graduated from college, found a job, and has just received his first paycheck.

The maple tree had been standing on the slope for seventy years.

The old woman in Intensive Care was on her last legs. She told the nurse that she had something important to tell him.

Juan was working at the convenience store cash register at 2 AM when six strange men walked in.

The four boys had been lost at sea for three days. They saw a ship a few kilometers away.

The hiker heard a noise in the underbrush. A boar was only ten meters away.

> One morning I shot an elephant in my pajamas.
>
> How he got in my pajamas, I'll never know.
>
> 喜劇演員／Groucho Marx

Chapter 25 訣竅五：字雅、句美、會說故事

若求文筆精簡，細讀左傳、唐詩。若要增韻律，唱詩經。

語言是聲音。書寫離不開聲音。文筆第一要訣是刪贅字，卻時而當加字。

我們在 Chapter 22「訣竅二：神助攻的私房書單」討論過 the Gettysburg Address。林肯經過幾年內戰，心思紛紜，倉促地寫出這篇；情況類似蘭亭集序、祭姪文稿，原是草稿，作者憑深厚的功夫瞬即而成，主觀意識沒太多干擾。渾然天成，不做作；沒有幾十年的醞釀，做不到的。放肆，要有條件。

撰文，多少需要那麼一點文彩、奇想。愛爾蘭劇作家 Richard Brinsley Sheridan（1751 – 1816）邀請一位年輕姑娘，Won't you come into the garden? I would like my roses to see you.

Walden 作者 Henry David Thoreau 精彩字句連連，如：Happiness is like a butterfly: the more you chase it, the more it will elude you. But if you turn your attention to other things, it will come and sit softly on your shoulder. 這是文采：奇想，而不做作。

請看看臺灣地名：嘉義、彰化、三義、宜蘭、花蓮、雲林、桃園，文學底子深厚，充滿詩意；「宜蘭」雖是 Kbalan 的譯音，卻譯得多雅！本猩剛來華時，路過羅東很困惑：羅西在哪？羅北呢？後來知道羅東原是rutong（猴子）的譯音，而「羅東」很合中文的基例。不然，宜蘭縣猴子鎮，饗喨唄。

Chapter 26 訣竅六：懂學術用語≠寫好文

Clear writing is clear thinking.

我們的時代崇尚科學。法治社會當然重視法律。所以很多教授，縱使自己專業不屬理工科技，盡量假裝很科學；寧犧牲文筆，也要寫的像法律文件。但每一篇文章必須寫那麼清楚、呆板、僵硬嗎？藝術是揀選。寫，恰到好處，須取捨：不寫死。

藝術，無有定法。有定法就不是藝術。

時下學術界的人盡其能事把文章寫的滯澀不通順，誤把滯澀當作深度、以囉唆為精準，讀起來極其痛苦，彷彿寫作的人希望沒有人願意看、煞讀者的興趣。如果寫的簡潔有力、順暢易讀，對不起指導教授。

倘若讀者還不知道本猩在說甚麼，一定沒讀過學術文章。「國際自傷行為研究學會於 2007 年宣稱 NSSI 須具有下列特性：(1) 重複性蓄意地對身體進行直接的傷害性動作且造成傷害。」這種文筆能看嗎？

這也牽涉到寫作的目的：如果心有所思，想表達，讓它人了解自己的想法、接受自己的觀點，務求文筆暢通、明瞭。

我讀過一篇英國現今哲學大師的文章，用西方哲學術語、結構，闡述人應該佈施的道理。我看了十幾頁，一點也沒有起佈施的念頭，看完只鬆一口氣：我終于走出來了！看完這篇，我沒想要捐一塊錢，只覺得作者很厲害，可以串那麼多術語，文字那麼多、內容那麼少。慈濟證嚴法師講話沒有嚴謹結構，可是多少人聽了就穿上白褲子，掏錢去做善事去了。寫作的目標是傳達內容或吹捧自我？

> **本猩案：這也與文化有關。**
> **法國人寫作的目的，確實是吹捧自我。**
> **法國文人說，英國人寫英文是要 express，法國人寫法文是要 impress.**

學仔（研究學術的水泥頭腦）面對術語，好比小狗得到骨頭：怎麼啃都不膩。討論專門領域，需要術語才能說交代清楚，是一回事；但不需要時，習慣把白話講成術語，愛用 jargon，這是騙人的，不是深度。學仔刻意寫的讓大家看不懂，取代思考、內涵。

學仔研討 personally occupied individual learning stations/ 個人佔據的個人學習崗位、manually activated transcribing instruments/ 手動抄錄儀器。請猜是啥？學生書桌、筆！

很多學仔太習慣學術文章，寫不出正常、雅緻的句子。舉例，呼籲學仔注意文筆，出現這句：Efforts should be made by scholars to avoid the utilization of jargon。讀者應該能看出文筆的拙劣。我們來修改：Scholars should avoid jargon. 十二字變成四字。如果要傳達訊息，當然要精簡扼要。

沒有人規定教授不可以寫人話吧。臺灣的學仔喜歡寫 aforementioned；不如寫 as I just mentioned，假如怕說道「我」招天譴，寫 as was just mentioned 亦可，又是學仔最愛的被動語氣。雖然字數增加，但沒有那麼做作。

寫學術文章不好嗎？除了美感盡失，有什麼不好呢？因為研究顯示，讀者閱讀學術文章，對科技失去興趣、不想進一步了解議題。不了解議題，民主國民如何投票？假如立法院討論食安、性別、原住民傳統領域、污染、氣候變遷、瘟疫等等種種重大問題，而一般民眾不了解其中的道理，沒興趣也沒信心探索，就很難建立公平、有競爭力的社會。

洋猩說文解字

床前看月光，
疑是地上霜，
舉頭望山月，
低頭思故鄉。

發現與小時候背的不太一樣嗎？因為這是最早的版本，依據北宋郭茂倩的「樂府詩集」。後來明朝人才暗插了兩個「明」字。看吧，學術不無聊，不要寫死就好了。

Practice Writing

Write a sentence for each of these words.

- scant
- recollect
- pretentious
- pitch
- pretend

Write an essay.

What country or culture would you like to learn more about? Give details. Be specific.

Lesson V
階段式實作練習

Chapter 27 練習寫金句
Time to Combine

Combine these elements into an essay. First think of how you are going to write your essay. What do you want to write? How will you write it? What is your first sentence? What is your ending?

You may like to find background information by asking people, going to a library, or searching online. However, you won't find anything online about playing bagpipes to buffalo; I made that up for fun.

Write as much or as little as you see fit.

1.

three day holiday / family together for a trip / 25 year old son driving / the father criticizes his driving / daughter, 29, doesn't want to get married / parents want grandchildren, are unhappy / the mother in denial /

denial: 逃避現實

2.

There are over 600 buffalos (American bisons) in the Witchita Mountains. A man went to play bagpipes for them. Why did he want to do that? What pieces did he play? What was their reaction?

3.

in the middle of a shower / strong earthquake / water stopped / power blackout / covered with soap / can't find clothes / building still swaying / hear things breaking

4.

This story took place eight hundred years ago. People living in a remote area knew little about the outside world. One day a man rode into their area on a horse. The oldest woman in the village was the only person who had ever seen a horse. The man carried a fine sword and four pieces of gold. Nobody knew what gold was.

5.

This story took place on a planet fifteen thousand lightyears away. An ulyarka, an animal living in the sea, was arguing with a vrabac, a flying animal with a bad reputation for not paying gambling debts. What were their names? What did they look like? They were both highly educated, but each thought the other was stubborn and unreasonable. What were they arguing about? What happened?

Chapter 28 去蕪存菁練出文章節奏

Into the Trashcan

Delete unnecessary or irrelevant sentences.

Passage 1: ice climbing

Although quite similar to rock climbing, ice climbing requires hand tools and crampons. (Crampons have ten or twelve points, and are attached to footwear to increase mobility on ice.) Unlike rock, ice changes throughout the day and throughout the season. Wearing crampons on rock damages them very quickly. On vertical ice, the climber stands with feet about shoulder-width apart and level, for a stable, comfortable stance. Then you reach up as high as you can and plant the pick of one ice tool into the ice. Ice is cold, so remember to dress warm. Some ice may come loose, so plant your tool a bit to the side, not directly over your face. Then plant the other one. Pull yourself up and step upward. Let your legs do the work, not your arms, or you will exhaust yourself. Continue upward. Center your balance below the planted tool as you remove and replace the other tool, or else you might come off the ice like a door opening.

Delete:

- Unlike rock, ice changes throughout the day and throughout the season.
- Wearing crampons on rock damages them very quickly.
- Ice is cold, so remember to dress warm.

Passage 2: control panel

The control panel has a very small monochrome LCD screen, menu navigation buttons, a keypad with eight buttons, and special buttons for copying and faxing. The buttons are somewhat small. Buttons also refer to those things you use to keep your shirt closed. I thought navigating the menus and settings on that tiny screen was tedious. I had to keep cleaning my glasses while I worked. The menu is kind of disorganized, so sometimes I had to refer to the printed guide to find what I wanted.

Delete:

- Buttons also refer to those things you use to keep your shirt closed.
- I had to keep cleaning my glasses while I worked.

宜字・字宜

最近看到這麼一面告示牌，叫捷運乘客怎麼到臺大醫院：

Disembark from the subway at the National Taiwan University Hospital (hereinafter referred to as NTUH) MRT stop.

寫這句的人顯然沒讀過多少英文。國際條約、訴訟狀子，也許可以厚著臉皮寫 hereinafter，但通俗文章不妥。Disembark 屬于時十九世紀的字眼，很少用。已說 get off the subway，所以 MRT 該刪。可以寫：

Get off the subway at the National Taiwan University Hospital (NTUH) stop.

Passage 3: grizzly bears

The grizzly bear (*Ursus arctos horribilis*) was listed as an endangered species in 1975. The Endangered Species Act of 1973 (16 USC § 1531 et seq) is the main law in the USA for protecting imperiled species of plants and animals. The Fish and Wildlife Service planned a recovery effort to build viable populations in places where the grizzly bear lived at the time of the listing. The North Cascades ecosystem is a large, contiguous habitat, but is isolated from grizzly bear populations elsewhere. There are black bears in this ecosystem, but they are a different species. Nobody knows for sure exactly how many grizzly bears live in this area, but most likely there are not enough to form a viable population. Grizzly bears reproduce slowly, which added to the problem. The Fish and Wildlife Service planned to reintroduce grizzly bears to this area, lest they disappear entirely. They are important links in the biodiversity of this ecosystem, and should be present for the benefit and enjoyment of people now and in the future. Wolves also contribute greatly to the health of ecosystems. Grizzly bears are also very important to tribal cultural and spiritual values. The public should be educated to understand the importance of grizzly bears, so that they will support the recovery program.

Delete:

- The Endangered Species Act of 1973 (16 USC § 1531 et seq) is the main law in the USA for protecting imperiled species of plants and animals.
- There are black bears in this ecosystem, but they are a different species.
- Wolves also contribute greatly to the health of ecosystems.

Passage 4: nuclear power

Many people believe that nuclear power is dangerous because of radiation, but worldwide, an average of two hundred people die from radiation each year. Compare that to the 4.2 million killed annually by air pollution, such as caused by thermal power plants. There has been great controversy about nuclear power plants, but they are undeniably safer than thermal or hydroelectric power plants. Some reservoirs are very deep. If they were not so deep, they would freeze in the winter. If you eat potato chips every day, you absorb more radiation than you would if you lived next to a nuclear power plant. The nuclear reactor at Fukushima had worked safely for forty years without incident, and was two weeks from retirement when struck by the 2011 earthquake. The death toll at Fukushima was due mostly to the evacuation of residents, which was done mainly for political reasons. Although many deaths were expected at Fukushima from cancer, even survivors of the atom bombing of Hiroshima and Nagasaki had only a 10% increase in cancer rate. If cancer were linked to radiation, people who live in places with naturally high background radiation, like Colorado, would have high cancer rates, but that is not the case. The radiation in Colorado is caused by high concentrations of uranium in the ground, but the state has some of the lowest cancer rates in the United States.

Delete:

- Some reservoirs are very deep.
- If they were not so deep, they would freeze in the winter.

Passage 5: Wrigley

As a young man selling soap in Chicago, William Wrigley Jr was so tenacious that one storeowner "admitted he would either have to give me an order or kill me, and he didn't want to kill me." Wrigley was born in Philadelphia and moved to Chicago. Chewing gum was usually given away free in those days, but Wrigley quickly realized its potential and entered the market. During the recession in 1907, other firms were cutting back on advertising. Wrigley mortgaged everything he had, and bought $1.5 million worth of advertising for $250,000. This campaign was so successful that Wrigley chewing gum became a national brand. In 1915, William Wrigley invented direct marketing by mailing complimentary sticks of Doublemint gum to 1.5 million households, every household listed in every phonebook in the United States. In Taiwan, flyers are mistakenly called DM, for direct marketing. This campaign was so successful that in 1919, gum was mailed to seven million households. Altogether, 26 million sticks of gum were sent. Wrigley continued advertising in the following decade by sending two sticks of chewing gum to every baby on their second birthday. The babies were too young to chew the gum, so their parents chewed it for them. Their ads appeared everywhere: on huge billboards, on taxis, and in subways. They set up a series of 17 billboards along the main railway running through New Jersey. Long distance buses were uncommon, and air travel practically unheard of, so most people traveled by train. In the late 1920s, Wrigley placed ads in the Sunday funny papers. The ads appeared in color. Wrigley bought the Chicago Cubs baseball team and renamed the stadium Wrigley

Field, further promoting his brand. During WWII, American soldiers were given gum to relieve tension and sore throats. The GIs used chewed gum to patch jeep tires, gas tanks, life rafts, and airplane parts. By then, Wrigley's advertising was so successful that chewing gum had become an American stereotype.

Delete:

- Wrigley was born in Philadelphia and moved to Chicago.
- In Taiwan, flyers are mistakenly called DM, for direct marketing.
- The babies were too young to chew the gum, so their parents chewed it for them.
- Long distance buses were uncommon, and air travel practically unheard of, so most people traveled by train.
- The ads appeared in color.

評：The ads appeared in color 可以併入前句：Wrigley placed color ads in the Sunday funny papers.

> The first and most important thing of all, at least for writers today, is to strip language clean, to lay it bare down to the bone.
>
> 美國作家／Ernest Hemingway

Practice Writing

Complete these sentences. Use your imagination. Try not to write something obvious. Think a bit.

The ancient boundary stone ________________

She refused to buy blood diamonds ________________

As the ship sailed northwest ________________

A green cucumber ________________

The car she wanted to buy ________________

Write a sentence for each of these words.

- resound
- legend
- relent
- cactus
- taper

Write an essay.

Describe an accomplishment that you are particularly proud of. Why did you do it? What obstacles did you encounter? How did you overcome them? Did anybody help you? How long did it take?

▶▶

Chapter 29 排列組合強化寫作組織力

Order out of Chaos

Place these sentences in order.

Passage 1: a microscope

❶ Any damage should be reported at once.

❷ Unwrap each piece and place it on a clean, dry, flat surface.

❸ Install the left stage plate.

❹ On receipt of this instrument, examine all parts carefully for possible damage in shipping.

❺ Tip the microscope base on its left side to find the coaxial stage screw mounts.

❻ Request an inspection of the damage.

❼ Gently tighten the screws using a flathead screwdriver.

❽ The parts of the microscope are packed in two Styrofoam containers, and the rest are wrapped in plastic.

❾ Set the base of the microscope on a firm, flat surface.

❿ When the coaxial stage has been mounted properly, lay the microscope base on its right side to find the screw holes for the left stage plate.

❹, ❶, ❻, ❽, ❷, ❾, ❺, ❼, ❿, ❸

Passage 2: tetherball

❶ Players hit the ball with their open hands, closed hands, or both hands.

❷ The players face each other, and have to stay on their own side of their court.

❸ One player hits the ball clockwise, the other counterclockwise.

❹ The ball may not be hit with any other part of the body.

❺ The player who first winds the rope all the way around the pole wins.

❻ Stepping off-side is against the rules.

❼ The court has two equal sides, one for each player.

❽ Any player who touches the rope immediately forfeits the game.

❾ To play tetherball, two opposing players strike a ball attached to a rope on a tall pole, and try to wind the rope all the way around the pole.

❿ Touching the rope is also against the rules.

⓫ Tetherball is an exciting game, a great workout, doesn't require much equipment, and doesn't take up much space.

❾，❼，❷，❻，❿，❽，❶，❹，❸，❺，⓫
解：⓫可置最後，亦可為首句。

Passage 3: beagles

Beagle 翻「米格魯」，完全走音。本猩提倡正音爲「皮狗」。養過的人一定了解。

❶ If you want a dog that is quiet and obeys commands instantly, don't get a beagle.

❷ A beagle is far from the easiest dog to train.

❸ Anybody who has a beagle will tell you that they can get into a lot of trouble, but even if they make you angry sometimes, they are warm, wonderful companions.

❹ With their big ears, soft eyes, and happy disposition, beagles are one of the most popular dog breeds.

❺ However, if you want a loving, understanding dog, get a beagle.

❻ If you want a dog that will jog obediently next to you, don't get a beagle.

❼ However, they are also infamous for being headstrong.

❽ If you want a dog that constantly keeps you laughing with its antics, get a beagle.

❾ They are noted for being friendly, strong, brave dogs that get along great with children.

❿ If you don't have space for your dog to run around, don't get a beagle.

❹，❾，❼，❷，❻，❶，❿，❺，❽，❸

評：❻、❶ 可對調。❺ 說 however，故排 ❽ 前爲妥。

Passage 4: lockdown

❶ They would bang out ideas, figure out how to word emails, and even decide what to wear.

❷ Some discovered that the constant chatter got on their nerves, and even told themselves to pipe down.

❸ During the coronavirus lockdowns of 2020, many people discovered they were talking to themselves.

❹ Maybe they didn't always talk out loud, but very often they would wander around the house muttering to themselves.

❺ Instead of remaining silent, they started talking to themselves.

❻ Although talking to yourself is usually frowned on, many say that it helped them cope with being alone at home for day after day.

❼ Some would give themselves motivational talks, to help them through the long hours.

❽ During difficult times, everybody needs a bit of reassurance, and if there's nobody there to give it, sometimes you just have to do it yourself.

❾ People were used to everyday conversation at work, but confined to home, they had nobody to talk to.

❿ If they had done this before, they had not been aware of it.

❸, ❿, ❾, ❺, ❹, ❻, ❼, ❶, ❷, ❽

評：前後文沒有明顯的因果關係，所以比較難排。❼、❶ 順序可調。❽ 可移 ❻ 後；但若如此移，末句弱，所以不移較好。

Passage 5: typhoons

❶ Typhoons form in parts of the ocean near the equator with warm sea surface temperature.

❷ When the Pacific is active, the Atlantic is normally quiet, and vice versa.

❸ The majority of typhoons form between June and November, although they can occur throughout the year.

❹ The northwest Pacific usually has the most and strongest typhoons.

❺ Although these conditions are necessary, they do not guarantee that a typhoon will form.

❻ Atmospheric instability and high humidity are also essential.

❼ The winds rotate around a center, called an eye.

❽ There is an inverse relationship between western Pacific typhoons and north Atlantic hurricanes.

❾ If the Coriolis effect is strong enough, a low pressure center forms.

❸，❶，❻，❺，❾，❼，❹，❽，❷，
評：❸、❶可以對調，但若然，❻的 also 突兀。

Practice Writing

Complete these sentences.

The crowd chased the ________

He jumped when he heard ________

When Samantha flubbed her lines ________

Procrastination ________

As far as we could see ________

Write a sentence for each of these words.

- undo
- coarse
- magnificent
- drastic
- demonstrate

Write an essay.

What is your favorite animal? Describe that animal. Explain why you like it.

▶▶

Chapter 30 挑不合宜句子練邏輯力 Odd Man Out

Delete any sentence that doesn't belong. There may be more than one.

Passage 1: Open, sesame

People around the world enjoy the Arabian Nights. Perhaps the most famous phrase from those stories is "Open, sesame!" In the story of Ali Baba and the Forty Thieves, the thieves store their loot in a magic cave in a mountain. The only way to open the door to the cave is by calling out the magic phrase, Open Sesame! The English word sesame is related to the Arabic *simsm*. But the question arises, why sesame? Why not banana, or yam, or eggplant? Ali Baba's greedy brother forgot the password and called out other plants, which doomed him. His brother was named Kasim, or Cassim. Babylonian magic used sesame oil, which shows that many people consider that sesame has magical properties. It seems that when the sesame plant ripens, the pods split open with an audible pop. This may be the inspiration for this phrase. Some people have said in jest that the phrase is "Open, says me," but this is obviously just a joke.

- The English word sesame is related to the Arabic *simsm*.
- His brother was named Kasim, or Cassim.
- Babylonian magic used sesame oil, which shows that many people consider that sesame has magical properties.
- Some people have said in jest that the phrase is "Open, says me," but this is obviously just a joke.

評：Ali Baba's greedy brother forgot the password and called out other plants, which doomed him 可留可刪。

Passage 2: the test

Kyle, Elijah, Jason, and Aaron had a big test in Introduction to Logic on Friday morning, but they heard about a big party at another fraternity on Thursday night, so they decided to go. It was a great party! They had such a good time that they lost track of the time until Aaron noticed the sky was getting light in the east. That meant that the night was almost over. They panicked, because they hadn't studied and were sure they would flunk their test. If they flunked their test, they would fail the course, too. They put their heads together and came up with a plan. They didn't change clothes. Instead, they went to a mudpuddle by the road and got all filthy. When they arrived at the test room, they told their teacher that they had been to a wedding the night before. On the way home, they ran over a nail and got a flat tire. They didn't have a spare and couldn't find a garage or gas station that was still open, so they had to push the car all the way back to their dormitory. They all lived in the same dormitory. They asked the teacher to postpone their test until Monday, and she agreed. She agreed that they could take the test on Monday. The boys were proud of themselves for pulling a fast one on the teacher. They cracked the books, and went to school Monday morning ready for their test. Their teacher said, "This is a Special Condition test. To take this test, you have to sit in separate classrooms." That was fine with the boys, because they were well prepared. That means they were ready for the test.

When they got their test papers, they found there were only two questions.

1. Name ______________________ (1 point)
2. Which tire ran over the nail? (99 points)
   A Front right
   B Front left
   C Back right
   D Back left

This is a very funny story.

- That meant that the night was almost over.
- If they flunked their test, they would fail the course, too.
- They all lived in the same dormitory.

評：已經說 their dormitory，所以此句該刪。

- She agreed that they could take the test on Monday.
- That means they were ready for the test.
- This is a very funny story. 若需要告知「這個好笑」，鐵定不好笑。

Passage 3: feminism

Feminism in the United States began in New England. But where did these radical ideas come from? The scholar Sally Roesch Wagner has documented one important source of inspiration: the powerful Iroquois Confederation of Amerindians. Many of the early feminists lived next to the Iroquois tribes in upstate New York; local newspapers reported on council meetings and spiritual ceremonies. The Iroquois hold similar meetings and ceremonies to this day. Women and men had equal voice in tribal government. The respect and authority in their families which Iroquois women enjoyed was far beyond anything comparable in White society.

- The Iroquois hold similar meetings and ceremonies to this day.

How many paragraphs should I write?

很多學生，尤其托福考生，問一篇文章要分幾段？甚至我看過老師劇烈爭論，托福作文寫四段才對？五段才對？

或許初學首次下筆，沒概念，可以建議寫四段或五段，但寫過兩三篇後，可以丟掉這種框架。各位，本書傳述英文寫作，不是八股文教材。要寫幾段，好比討論高一學生要穿幾號鞋子：因人而異。一段是一個主題、一個 main idea；若不知如何分段，大約五六句分段吧。每段第一句是 main idea，接下闡述、舉例、輔助、證明。段落太長，讀者辛苦，喘不過氣；眼睛也疲勞。偶寫一句段落，可改文章節奏，但常用，氣短，全文難連貫，仿若「湊頁數」而非「作」文。

Practice Writing

Complete these sentences. Use your imagination. Try not to write something obvious. Think a bit.

The Irishman felt his pale skin burning under Taiwan's hot sun as ___________

Watching as seventeen gigantic spaceships emerged from behind the moon, __________

Since the stone marker dividing their lots __________

Seeing the police car's lights in the rear view mirror, __________

With a run of bad luck, she __________

Write a sentence for each of these words.

- portray
- downfall
- prominence
- unauthorized
- nefarious

Write an essay.

What do you use your thumb for? Give details, tell a story, amuse your reader.

Chapter 31 句型重組弄懂脈絡架構
Order and Delete

Put these sentences in order. Delete unnecessary sentences.

Passage 1: a WWI hero

1. Johnson was a small man, 5 foot four inches tall, and weighed about 130 pounds.
2. They were sent to France, but at first saw little combat.
3. He was called Black Death, and became a hero at home and in France, but because he was black, the Army did not officially recognize his valor.
4. In other words, he was about 162 centimeters tall, and weighed under 60 kilograms.
5. Johnson threw grenades and shot his rifle, but quickly ran out of ammunition.
6. Suddenly, dozens of German soldiers charged out of the forest with bayonets fixed.
7. In the hand-to-hand fight over the next hour, using nothing more than a bolo knife, Johnson killed four German soldiers and wounded at least 24.
8. The German soldiers tried to drag him away as a prisoner, but Johnson stopped them.

❾ Guarding a bridge in the Argonne Forest in France in the early hours of May 14, 1918, William Henry Johnson heard some strange sounds.

❿ Penicillin had not been discovered yet, so many soldiers died from infections.

⓫ Roberts was wounded almost immediately.

⓬ Finally, in June, 2015, President Barack Obama posthumously awarded Johnson the Medal of Honor in a ceremony at the White House.

⓭ In June, 1917, William Henry Johnson enlisted in the 369th Infantry Regiment, based in Harlem.

⓮ The 369th was an all-black regiment commanded by mostly white officers, including their commander, Colonel William Hayward.

⓯ Johnson received 21 wounds in the fray.

⓰ He roused his partner, Needham Roberts, who thought Johnson was just nervous, and went back to sleep.

刪：❶、❹、❿
組：⓭、⓮、❷、❻、⓰、❾、⓫、❽、❺、❼、⓯、❸、⓬

Passage 2: the elevator pitch

1. Keep your ideas concise, clear, and easy to understand.
2. The story goes that Michael Caruso, an editor at *Vanity Fair*, was continuously trying to pitch story ideas to the Editor in Chief, but she was always too busy to sit down and listen.
3. Caruso would catch her while she was taking the elevator, and try to persuade her then.
4. An elevator ride lasts only a minute or two, so Caruso knew he had to condense his ideas and present the most important points very attractively.
5. A famous opera star was named Caruso, but that was Enrico Caruso.
6. Something that is irrelevant means it is not to the point.
7. This is what is called the Elevator Pitch.
8. If you have an idea to pitch, leave out the flowery rhetoric, and let the statistics wait.
9. Decision makers now are busy and don't have time to listen to long-winded discussions.
10. Get to the point, without a lot of irrelevant nonsense.
11. The first commercial elevator in New York City was installed in 1857.

⓬ Rock climbers call the length of a climbing rope a pitch, too.

⓭ A fancy word for long-winded is loquacious, or verbose.

⓮ Pitch here means a sales talk, not like pitching in baseball, or the pitch which is like tar.

組：❷，❸，❹，❼，❻，❽，❿，❶
刪：❺，❾，⓫，⓬，⓭，⓮

People who don't have nightmares don't have dreams. If you will excuse me, I have an appointment with myself to sit on the front steps and watch some grass growing.

美國作家／Robert Paul Smith

Passage 3: Sesame

❶ The Indian Subcontinent takes its name from the Indus River.

❷ Excavations of the Egyptian pharaoh Tutankhamen uncovered baskets of sesame among other grave goods, which tells us that sesame was present on the Nile by 1350 BCE.

❸ By two thousand years ago, sesame had entered China from the west, as shown by its original Chinese name, 胡麻 , barbarian hemp, and was widely cultivated.

❹ By the Tang and Sung dynasties, sesame oil was essential to everyday life, and continues to be so even now.

❺ Akkadian, one of the languages written in cuneiform, is the earliest documented Semitic language.

❻ Archeological discoveries indicate that sesame was domesticated in the Indian subcontinent at least 5500 years ago.

❼ The Iron Age kingdom of Urartu, in modern day Armenia, cultivated sesame at least 2750 years ago.

❽ With one of the highest oil contents of any seed, sesame seed is one of the oldest oilseed crops known.

❾ Chinese used sesame oil not only as food and medicine, but also to light lamps and, before the invention of gunpowder, for incendiary arrows.

⓾ The Indus Valley civilization exported sesame oil to Mesopotamia as long ago as 2000 BCE.

⓫ Urartu, also known as the Kingdom of Van, is important in modern Armenian nationalism, because the people of that kingdom spoke Armenian.

⓬ The oldest record of sesame is in a cuneiform document written 4000 years ago that describes presenting offerings of sesame liquor to the gods.

⓭ As a matter of fact, the English word "sesame" comes from the word šamaššammû, meaning "oily seed" in the ancient Mesopotamian language, Akkadian.

⓮ The ancient Greek geographer and historian, Herodotus, wrote that sesame was cultivated 3500 years ago in the region of the Tigris and Euphrates in Mesopotamia.

⓯ Many Armenian Americans live in California, especially in the Central Valley.

組：❽，❻，⓾，⓬，⓭，⓮，❷，❼，❸，❾，❹
刪：❶，❺，⓫，⓯
評：此篇依時序，所以容易排。

Passage 4: Slamaw

❶ Partly the Japanese wanted the Taiwanese to submit, and partly they wanted Taiwan's valuable timber, especially camphor.

❷ Official reports by the Japanese Governor General showed that the Japanese killed about 400,000 Han Chinese in the first twenty years of their rule.

❸ A few hundred Tayal of Slamaw fought off thousands of Japanese soldiers.

❹ Only four hunters survived, because they had been hunting in the mountains at the time of the Japanese atrocity.

❺ Once the entire village was inside, the Japanese nailed the doors shut, poured gasoline on the houses, and burned everybody in the entire village alive, young and old.

❻ They established a village called Kbayaw, and in 1920, invited the Tayal to a feast inside some new houses.

❼ Indigenous tribes ferociously resisted the Japanese invasion.

❽ When the Japanese Occupation of Taiwan began in the late 19th century, Taiwan had a population of some 2.5 million.

❾ Taiwan has about fifty species of camphor trees.

❿ The houses were newly built.

⓫ After years of war, the Japanese finally told the Tayal they wanted to stop fighting.

⓬ The Tsou made their peace with the Japanese, but the neighboring Bunun fought for decades, and were subdued only after numerous Japanese atrocities.

Slamaw 的中文名字是梨山。Tayal 是泰雅族；Tsou， 鄒；Bunun，布農。

組：❽，❷，❼，❶，⓬，❸，⓫，❻，❺，❹
刪：❾，❿
評：⓬ 勉強可以放最後，但文章就沒有重點、沒有完結感。

Practice Writing

Complete these sentences. Give your imagination free play. Be sure to write something vivid.

Planting potatoes was such a joy for Jonathan ________________

As the alligator approached ________________

She could still hear the sounds of the party ________

The archeologists studying the ancient, controversial inscription, "Made in Taiwan," discussed ________________

Returning home after twenty five years, ________________

Write a sentence for each of these words.

- impatient
- retract
- project
- enlarge
- ahead

Write an essay.

Learn about the *Book of Kells*. Write about it.

Chapter 32 一個題目寫多種版本練文藻
Try, Try, and Try Again

Revise and rewrite these paragraphs.

Make sure the grammar is correct, the words are used correctly, and (everybody sing along with me!) omit unnecessary words!

Passage 1: the waiting room

When you come into the waiting room, you see a few seats. The seats are there for people to sit in. There is a desk. A lady sits there. She is the receptionist. She has a big desk. The desk has a telephone and a computer on it. The desk has some pens, some pencils and some paper on it. The telephone is black. The floor is clean. The walls are clean. Probably somebody cleans the office, maybe they have cleaners who come in and clean the office. There are pictures on the walls. They look like they are photographs, so yeah, I guess they probably are photographs! They are framed. The photos have lots of colors in them. One of them is not hanging down right, one side is a little crooked! Probably someone forgot to check to see if it straight. Its not. I'm not sure if the cleaners are supposed to look out for stuff like that. That picture is a picture of a ship in the water. It is a sailing ship. It is sailing across the ocean. Maybe the ship is going somewhere. But it's not going anywhere, it's just hanging on the wall of this office.

People don’t have anything to do there!!

They are waiting.

They look at the pictures. There’s a window. Some of the people look out the window. They try not to look at each other. They didn’t have cellphones when this story takes place, so they couldn’t look at Facebook or Instagram, because those weren’t invented yet. People didn’t have computers in those days. They hadn’t been invented yet. There are a bunch of magazines. The magazines are on a coffee table by the seats. Sometimes people picking up the magazines and flip through them, not really reading them, just flipping through because they don’t have anything better to do and they don’t want to look at the photographs and they don’t want to look at the other people. The magazines have been there for a long time. you can tell they aren’t new, because I bet a lot of people have read them.

寫作的訣竅無它，就是修了再改、改了再修。朱熹臨終前一天，還把「大學章句」第一章注「實其心之所發，欲其一于善而無自欺也」的「一于善」改爲「必自慊」。

他如果多活幾年，一定有其它字要改。在此提供的範文，只不過是一種寫法，下文僅供參考。不要把範文當枷鎖。

參考範文

The receptionist in the waiting room sat at a big desk with a black telephone and some stationery. Colorful framed photographs decorated the walls. A photo of a ship at sea hung askew, as if seasick. The waiting people looked at the pictures or out the window. They tried not to look at each other. Some of them picked up the dogeared, well-thumbed magazines on the coffee table to browse.

評：英文的時態很美，要用。

這篇很難改，因為前後文不一致：當時到底有沒有電腦？ Receptionist 桌上有電腦嗎？有座位，可以不提，理所當然 waiting room 有座位、座位是給人家坐的。地板、牆壁乾淨，很正常，若沒有必要，不要提；髒地板才可能要指出。

沒事不要亂加驚嘆號！

誰整理辦公室，離題，刪。

Maybe the ship is going somewhere. But it's not going anywhere, it's just hanging on the wall of this office. 漂亮。要留要刪，須看下文方向而決定。如果要強調等待的人浪費生命在辦公室，可以留。

通常一段不要少于三句。可以長短相參，富有變化；要斟酌，但不要太常用單句段落。

Its、it's 須分清楚。
It's = it is 或 it has，其他用 its。

Passage 2: Richard's retirement party

Because Richard retiring, therefore the company planning to hold party honor him. They kept secret. Preparing for party, boss was asked say a speech. Boss takes money out of own pocket and tells people in the company to buy champagne, she want champagne so everybody can drink in Richard's honor. Last Monday is Richard's last day, so at the time that it is Monday, she tells Richard problem want to talk over for him, so use time for lunch and talk about the problem while they can eat lunch. This is secret, because they party at lunch. Everybody pay a bit money for buying a gift Richard. Richard liking play the chess. People buy special chess set so he memorize. All people of office go restaurant before Richard goes there, they hiding in kitchen. Kitchen very hot, food cooked there, maybe ovens and stove very, very hot. The people of office they hiding in kitchen when waiter tell them they all come out and Richard surprising. Boss she say speech she thanking Richard because Richard work very hard for long time. Then the staffs gifted Richard with chess set, Richard very very happy he maybe wants to cry. Boss bring champagne, everybody take glass and drank champagne for honor Richard. We are all very happy. Linda she cries, she always cry, after few years she retired too.

參考範文

Last Monday was Richard's last day on the job before he retired, so the company prepared a surprise party in his honor. The boss was asked to give a speech. She donated money to buy champagne for everybody to toast Richard. Since Richard loves chess, everybody chipped in to buy him a special commemorative chess set. On Monday morning, the boss told Richard she had a problem to discuss with him over lunch. All the people from the office got to the restaurant first and hid in the kitchen. At the waiter's signal, they all rushed out and surprised Richard. The boss gave her speech, thanking Richard for his hard work and long service. Then his co-workers presented Richard with the chess set; he was moved almost to tears. The boss produced the champagne, and everybody lifted their glasses to toast him. Everybody was happy, but as usual, Linda cried. She is due to retire in a few years.

評：原文時態一團糟，字彙需要加強。Because 或 therefore，選一，不可同時併用。全篇首句 because 起頭，很弱。餐廳廚房熱，不相干，刪。

Passage 3: punching

A good punch stems from rotating your hips. It's as if you tried to swing a baseball bat with just your arms and without moving your hips, you wouldn't have a very powerful swing. It's just like that when you hit with just your fist.

At the start of the punch, your foot should rotate around the ball of the foot that is in back of you so your fist has more power. If you rotate too much, you might fall over or you might lose your balance, whereas if you don't rotate enough, you might not get much power into that punch, per the case of hitting with the aforementioned baseball bat. Your legs and feet should push your arm forward, you push off that foot that is in back, you move your hips, and your arms flies straight to your target. Don't lift your elbow like you're trying to fly, because you're not a chicken, and don't do those big, slow roundhouse punches you only see in the movies. Don't throw your arm out too far, or else you might fall forward, and that's not a good thing to happen. Also, throwing your arm out too far is not good for your elbow.

參考範文

Rotating your hips is the foundation for a good punch. Imagine swinging a baseball bat with just your arms and shoulders, but without swiveling your hips: there would be little power in that swing. The same holds true for punching.

When you begin the punch, pivot your back foot on the ball for greater thrust. Don't pivot so much that you lose your balance, but make sure your punch draws the power of your legs. Don't throw those big, slow roundhouses that work only in movies. Punch straight, keeping your elbow down. Don't overextend your arm, to avoid injuring your elbow or losing your balance.

評：除非per hour, per kilogram，當「每」，不要寫per；不要當作「以」、「依據」、「由」。

Passage 4: corporate blather

The governing body of this corporation are in agreement as to the proposed financial mechanism, based on the complicit understanding that said moneys will be appropriated for utilization in adherence with the basic values and principles laid out in the funding allocation as per identified in said document.

參考範文

The Board approved the budget.

Practice Writing

Complete these sentences. Use your imagination.

She struggled with kleptomania for years __________

When I saw the hole in my umbrella, ____________________

Returning home from the wars, the soldier __________

The skunk walked calmly into the classroom __________

The poor service in the restaurant ____________________

Write a sentence for each of these words.

- inedible
- indelible
- ineligible
- illegible
- unintelligible

Write an essay.

What is the closest tree to where you are now? Take a close look at that tree. Do you know what kind it is? Describe it. Where does it grow? Is anybody taking care of it? How big is it? What does it look like? Have you seen its fruit?

Chapter 33 自我挑戰看題寫作

Now It's Your Turn

Write an essay with each of these topics. 注意第一句、章法。如何敘述？鋪陳？收尾？

Note:

These are just suggestions to help you get going. You can add or subtract as much as you like. Write as much or as little as you like, but each piece should be complete.

Use these words; they don't all have to go into the same piece.

- flip
- flop
- check
- yield
- dawdle
- feeble
- colossal
- gaunt
- strut
- intrinsic

Passage 1:

Write about something that happened to you when you were in elementary school.

Passage 2:

Write about a toothache or a headache.

Passage 3:

Write about somebody you work with. If you are a student, write about someone you go to school with.

Passage 4:

Write about what it must be like to be 215cm tall. Think of the advantages and disadvantages. Do you want to discuss this objectively or write a story?

Passage 5:
Write about jet lag, getting carsick, or insomnia.

Passage 6:
If you like sports and exercise, write about that. If you don't, explain your standpoint. In either case, be as convincing as possible.

Passage 7:
Who was Richard Smalls? When did he live? What did he do? What is he famous for? The person you want lived in the 19th century and has something to do with Charleston harbor.

Passage 8:
Write about the view from your home. What can you see? How far can you see? Have you ever seen anything unusual? Do you like your view? If you wanted to improve it, how would you change it?

Passage 9:
Write about your strangest experience shopping, traveling, on vacation, or at work.

Passage 10:
Write about something frustrating that happened to you. Explain what led to it, why it frustrated you, and how you dealt with it.

Chapter 34 看圖說故事練想像力 Write from Pictures

Use Google Images to search for each of these themes. Write about the fifth picture you find for each key word. You may have to read up on the theme. You can describe the picture, make up a story, or write whatever you please. Write as much or as little as you like. Be lively, descriptive, and specific. Do not be predictable, boring, or vague. Work for variety; vary your format, approach, style, and attitude.

Remember to date your work, and revise, rewrite, and revise.

Be sure to use these words; they don't all have to go into the same piece.

- submarine
- unfettered
- recognize
- home
- memory
- pretend
- diplomatic
- pandemonium
- bristle
- skateboard

Theme 1: elephant

Theme 2: Puerto Williams, Chile

Theme 3: Sutton Hoo

Theme 4: Hieronymus Bosch

Theme 5: baby gorilla

Theme 6: jousting

Theme 7: the Carrington Event

Theme 8: the liberation of Auschwitz

Theme 9: saddle shoes

Theme 10: fudge

> No one will ever lose a reader, no matter how difficult the subject, by writing agreeably, with good humor, with an effort of informality.
>
> 歷史學家／Bernard deVoto

Lesson VI
實用範例說明

▶▶

Chapter 35 商業書信：Let's Get Down to Business

想像：你是 Milena Cipelejović，擔任跨國公司 Miseve, Inc 採購部門的經理，天天要看兩三百封 emails。以下這兩封，哪一個比較有吸引力？

A.

Dear Sir/Madam，

We have obtained your esteemed name and address from an online business directory。we hear much about your prestigious company。It is grae honor have this opprotnity to do business with you're noted company. We are sure this will be a salaciously profitable relationship that will mutually benefitus to great profit and advantage，Wee look forward to many year very lucrative relationship between your esteemed company and our humble company。 so would like totake this opportunity for introduce ourselves。 Alow me to indtroduce my humble company .Please be advised that we‘re a famous trading company in Taiwan specializing in import and export。 We offer the best pricesand are eager to engage in trading with your famous trading company。We have the honor to send to you our catalogue for your honored perusal。you will find that we offer the most highest quality for the most

lowest rpices。We look forward toyour speedy response, kindly respond as quickly as possible so ew can engage in a very, very profitable and lucrative busyness relationship 。We shall be obliged you kindly sned us irrevocable L/C at your earliest convenient so we begin to starting make mutual money。

B.

Dear Ms Cipelejović:

Trade reports show that Miseve, Inc. is a major supplier of mouse shoes in North America. Our company, Yamin Qoli, has fifteen years' experience producing shoes for pet mice.

- We offer mouse shoes in black, pink, yellow with green polka dots, and orange with fuchsia stripes.
- Our mouse shoes come in a wide variety of styles and sizes.
- We can custom make mouse shoes to meet your requirements.
- We provide mouse shoes in 1.8mm waterproof suede microfiber, polyvinyl chloride, or ISO20345 standard microfiber PU leather, with rubber or polyester soles.
- We can produce up to 600 sets of mouse shoes a day, to be shipped in 20 or 40 foot containers.
- Enclosed please see our schedule of prices.

Best regards,
Bartholomew Oobleck
Manager
oobleck@yaminqoli.com
Yamin Qoli, Inc
Fanglin, Changhua, Taiwan

請讀者不要懷疑，本猩看過一簍筐像 A 的信件，真實不虛：中文字型寫外文、中文標點、錯字百出、用詞不當、廢話連篇、空泛、沒有重點。沒聽過美國商人的口頭禪嗎？ Time is money. 沒有人要看長篇大論。寫商業書信，白刀直入：Get to the point! 現在是廿一世紀，不要用一堆十九世紀的客套話，除非希望對方認為你做生意食古不化。

舉例：中文很多範本寫 the sixteenth of this month，囉唆！ July 16.

我們來看看廿一世紀那些用法適合或不適合。

👎 kindly

宜：please

👎 Please be advised

例：Please be advised that the shipment is on the way.

改：The shipment is on the way.

👎 Kindly advise

宜：tell us, let us know, inform us

例：Kindly advise when your representative will arrive.

改：Please tell us when your representative will arrive.
Let us know when your representative will arrive.

👎 I am writing this email for the purpose of

例：I am writing this email to enquire if you could kindly provide us with the prices for Model 233.

改：Please quote prices for Model 233.

👎 your famous company, your esteemed company

直接刪除或寫公司名號；依需亦可寫 your company.

👎 in (with) reference to, above-captioned, above-mentioned, above referenced

宜：about, concerning

例：In reference to your message dated the 16th of June, I would like to take this opportunity to explain the situation as it stands as of this date.

改：The current situation of the problem you discussed in your message of June 16 is...

例：I am writing in reference to your above referenced inquiry, dated the sixteenth of June.

改：Concerning your inquiry of June 16,

👎 We shall be obliged if you...

宜：We would you like you to, We would appreciate it if you...

例：We shall be obliged if you call to our attention reputable suppliers with whom we may have the honor of engaging in trade.

改：We would appreciate it if you could introduce some suppliers we can do business with.

👎 Please do not hesitate to contact me

改：Please call me, please notify me, please tell me, please let me know，please 可刪。除非有明確的事情可能需要討論，不要寫 please call me 之類的咄咄逼人字句。舉例：依需可寫 Please call me as soon as the bank notifies you about the delayed payment 之類的具體事件，但 Please do not hesitate to contact me if you have any questions，不用寫。

Enclosed please find

宜：I have enclosed, XXX is enclosed

例：Enclosed please find three copies of the contract.

改：I have enclosed three copies of the contract.
Three copies of the contract are enclosed.

For your perusal

例：Enclosed please find our latest catalogue for your perusal.

改：Our latest catalog is enclosed.

Under separate cover

宜：I am sending you separately

例：I am sending you three copies of the contract under separate cover.

改：I am separately sending you three copies of the contract.
I am FedExing you three copies of the contract.
I am messengering you three copies of the contract.

At your earliest convenience

改：As soon as possible, as soon as you can，但猶須斟酌。需要這樣逼人嗎？

in compliance with your request

宜：as you requested

Please note that

例：Please note that the shipment has been slowed due to the recent typhoon.

改：The recent typhoon slowed the shipment.

I am looking forward to hearing from you soon. 刪。憑啥逼人呢？沒禮貌。

We are desirous of

宜：we want to, we plan to

例：We are desirous of extending our market in your prestigious country.

改：We plan to improve our market share in (國名).

We hope to improve our sales in (國名).

本猩招供：這句 desirous of 我真的沒學過，在中文出版的英文商業書信指南才看到的，瞬間感到一股陰霉的腐氣。

商業書信分兩大類：紙本、email。

email

Subject line 簡單明瞭，容易引起對方興趣。
對方每天收到多少 emails ？多數是 spam 垃圾信件，見即刪，不讀。
Subject line 寫的不好，對方速刪不開。忌空泛，利明確。Subject line 拼錯字，可以不寄，對方不開，見即丟垃圾桶。

錯誤示範：

Subject: about your order

改：Subject: attn Mr Oobleck, mouse shoe order #BS20YQ41559383
attn：attention，注意。可以刪。

錯誤示範：

Subject: important information about your order

改：不要吊人胃口。很多詐欺 email 就是用 important information 這種 subject。
Subject: attn Ms McBoing, freighter sank, cargo lost

Email 自動注明日期，但還是要寫。寫在抬頭下，置左、置中、置右。亦可寫在簽名下。但日期必與簽名對齊。

Email 第一行是稱呼，招呼。最好寫成
Dear Mr Oobleck:
Dear Ms Azdaja:
Dear Dr Zmaj:
收件人稱謂、姓後加冒號，私人信件才用逗號。（千萬不可把對方姓名拼錯！

寫錯對方姓名是沒禮貌的笨蛋。姓名越難拼的人越在乎。）
要不要這樣？
To Whom It May Concern:
Dear Sir/Madam:

簡單說，NO!
許多老派的商業寫作顧問以為 To Whom It May Concern 還很響唬，但一般八十歲以下的人認為太老套、發霉發臭了。
寫信，到底在乎不在乎誰看？隨便，給工友、警衛看也可以？這個年代，寫 To Whom It May Concern 等同通知收信人，寫的人很懶、死腦筋、不了解潮流。

很多美國大學表明，To Whom It May Concern 起頭的申請資料、推薦函等等，一律拒收：沒禮貌。

網路英文教學還有人推薦 Gentlemen: 大概不想做生意吧。
至少，Dear Sir/Madam: 已經進步到二十世紀後半。但無情無趣。
寫信，到底給誰看？ 上公司網站、看他們的臉書、到 LinkedIn 找、用 Gmail 的 Rapportive 查收件人尊姓大名。萬一還找不到，乾脆打電話問！
"Hello, I saw you're looking for a Full Stack Developer at Yamin Qoli, and I'm the person for that job, so I'm applying, and I'd like to know the name of the person in charge of hiring. Could you please tell me who that is?" "Could you spell that for me?"

千萬不可拼錯對方姓名！

如果真查不出姓名，寫部門：Dear Sales Manager、Dear Hiring Manager 之類。總比 To Whom 或 Dear Sir/Madam 好一百倍。
那麼，To Whom It May Concern 絕對不可以用嗎？如果想與對方保持距離，例如申訴、告訴，可以寫。

再強調一次：稱呼後加冒號，不可用逗點！

跟對方已經算熟，或者不正式的信函，可以寫 Greetings、Hello，甚至 Hi。帥氣的稱呼，可以用逗點。要十足把握才可寫此格。若有疑問，記得：禮多，人不怪。

第一句，不要講到 we。重點放在對方；頭一字用 we 或 I，失敗在望！

第一句要積極、正面。很簡單的一招，Thank you for your email of May 25 或 Thank you for your quick reply to my email of May 12 之類。如果與對方熟，可以寫 I hope your week is going well 之類的話。

董董懂噹噹噹

想像：

你有方案，想說服董淑美董事長，但董董很忙，抽不出時間。

你坐捷運，遇到董董，她在下一站下車，你只有這個機會讓董董懂。時間不到一分鐘，要讓董董眼睛一亮，噹噹噹！你的方案可行！

寫商業書信、申請函、申請學校、推薦函等等，都要記得這個原則。

算了，我們這樣說：寫信，除了情書、家書，都要記得董董懂噹噹噹！

在英文叫做 elevator pitch，
因為原來場景在電梯，
換到捷運，不是一樣嗎？

有話快說！參考上文給 Ms Cipelejović 的信。

若報告壞消息，前後還是要寫正面的：

Thank you for your email (May 22). I am afraid delivery of your order #ABC12345 will be delayed until July, because Gebenimas Freight just informed us that pirates hijacked the container ship Nelaimingas yesterday (May 21) morning as it neared Singapore. Fortunately, all the crew are safe, but the cargo has disappeared and it will take us until July to replace it.

Attached to this email, I am sending a file with a complete report, along with insurance claims. I have also sent hard copies of the complete report to your office by express mail; you will receive them tomorrow.

I apologize for this unfortunate delay in our plans, but assure you that we will get you your merchandise as soon as humanly possible, and that our business cooperation will continue to prosper.

需要說明嗎？不可全大寫；大寫小寫依規矩。WRITING WITH ALL CAPITALS IS VERY RUDE AND IT SEEMS LIKE YOU'RE SHOUTING AND NOBODY WILL WANT TO DO BUSINESS WITH YOU.

最後祝福，選一：
Sincerely,
Best regards,
Kind regards,

Best,
All the best,
Cheers,
老寫法是 Sincerely yours 或 Yours sincerely，但我們人身自由，我不是你的奴僕，我不是 yours。除非寫給很老的商人，或頭腦很老化的商人，不要寫 yours。

Sincerely, Best regards, Kind regards, 都算正式。Best，All the best，Cheers，比較不正式，而親切。夠熟的話，平輩可用；假如一般職員寫給總經理、董事，不妥。

年輕人最喜歡 Cheers，也最快回信。
若已經合作一段時間，可以寫 As ever。
有人認為 Take care 親切，有人感到威脅，所以還是不要用。
Thx, Rgrds 限十三歲以下用。

寫給高級政府官員、宗教人士，可以寫 Respectfully。

Looking forward to hearing from you，幹嘛把對方逼得那麼緊？
千萬不要寫 Love。這，我需要說嗎？
也不要寫 sent from my iPhone。

網路很多商業書信的範本，文法不通、拼音不對、中式標點、陳腔濫調，可真誤人子弟。

再來，寫自己的名字，提行，寫頭銜，依需再提行註明公司資料：不加句點！

Sincerely,

Milo Juster
Editor
此處可加 Linkedin profile URL

Best regards,
Samantha Howells
Manager
Furniture Department
Max & Spender, Isle of Man

寫完了嗎？好，從頭再讀一遍，確定沒有打錯字、意思清楚、沒有廢話、沒有打錯字、文法通順、沒有錯字、字都打對了。對方姓名拼對嗎？要不要請同事過目？確定無誤，才按 send。

衡量你公司的性質：誰規定 **email** 必須用黑字？

律師、會計師、保險、銀行業者當然要黑字，表示很拘謹、規矩。但設計師？用黑字，是否表示沒有設計感、不願踰越老成矩？廣告、建築、攝影、娛樂業者可以選一種顏色，email 統一用此色，保證收件者印象深刻。甚至以後看到此色字體，聯想貴公司。建議用深色。螢光綠（#39FF14）好看，可是用此色寫信，傷眼睛。

需要強調嗎？自己的 email address 也要注意。十四歲申請的 sexybabygirl@doper 、universehero@idiot 不可用。

紙　本

現在一般通訊用 email，寄紙本屬特殊情形。因此，要考慮紙的品質。現在用以前的超薄紙，太寒酸；80gsm 可以用，100gsm 到 120gsm 剛好。信封與信紙要同款。

紙張一定要純白嗎？看公司的性質。一旦決定，不要常換。慎選字型，請參考 Chapter 13。選了，不要常換。用公司、單位信紙：印公司名稱、地址、聯絡方式等等。

Gorillaholic, Inc
123 Banana Drive,
Yungay District, Lotung, Taiwan ROC
886-000-000-000
gorillaholic.bnns.cd
snortsnarl@gorillaholic.bnns.cd

寫日期很重要。寫在抬頭下，置左、置中、置右。亦可寫在簽名下。但日期必與簽名對齊。寫收信人的姓名，提行；職位，提行；公司、地址；靠左。

Ms Amelia Cyfeillgar,
Manager, Footwear Department
Oinetakoak International
123 Turtlewax Street
Chicago, Illinois 60622
USA

空一行，稱呼，同 email。內容寫法與 email 一樣，且記：盡量一面寫完，還要留空簽名。若沒有必要而寫到第二頁，對方討厭你。少寫廢話！！

分段，兩種方法：一是 indent 縮排，每段首句前空五格，或 tab 一次。一是不縮排，每段用空行分。現在空行稍多些；選哪一個，均可，但用法要一致。結尾祝福，同 email。

祝福下空四行，打自己大名。不可畫線！只有合同、罰單、簽收才畫線。姓名後，沒有標點。

簽名要用黑筆簽；藍筆表示不重視、隨便；紅筆、綠筆表示未成年。建議花點錢買好的墨水筆（fountain pen），灌全黑墨，簽名要用這支。

再來是職位。如果上面沒有，此處寫 email、電話號碼。

不要把對方當白癡。不要註明 **email 或 ph**（美國通常用 ph，要小寫；TEL 比較中式。）下列左邊是錯誤示範，右為正確範例。

Yours sincerely,

____

Karen Zapovednicka.
Manager!
email: zapo@donkeyworld.com
PH: 123-1234-12345 ext. 450

Sincerely,
Amelia Cyfeillgar
Manager
cyfeillgar@naga.co.uk
12-123-1234-12345x450
(x450 轉分機 450)

如果對方頭腦那麼不清楚，看不出 cyfeillgar@naga.co.uk 是 email，不用跟他們做生意吧！

How to do it wrong
What's wrong with this business letter? Get out your pen and fix this mess.

Mitchell's Doughnuts

123 1st Avenue
NYC
TEL: 02302020

February 30, 2023

to: Donald's Bakery
Mr Donald Drumpf
725 5th Avenue
NYC.

Dear Donald,

We cannot provide you with any more doughnuts because of yoru terrible credit! We have unpaid accounts from you dating back since we started doing business with you, in 2016. If you want us to provide any more doughnuts for you, it has to be cash on the barrel.
We are sorry for any inconveniene this may cause you, but if you can save yourself from bankruptcy, and stay out of jail, maybe you can do business with us again! Please do not hesitate to call us if you have any questions.

Sincerly yours ,

____

Moskva Mitchell,
owner.

What's wrong? A lot.

- TEL 是中式英文，不用寫。
- 日期與簽名不齊。
- 勿寫 to:
- NYC 後不加標點。需寫 zip code。
- 商業書信稱謂後加冒號；逗點用于私人通訊。
- 第一段寫三個 we、一個 us；第二段寫一個 we、一個 us，重點放在自己。
- 商業書信、推薦函等不用驚嘆號。
- Your、inconvenience、sincerely 都拼錯，非常不專業。開 Word 的拼音檢查！
- 兩段間分行。
- 第二段首尾兩句很沒有誠意。不要寫客套話。
- 簽名空四行，不畫線。姓名後不加標點。逗點前不空格。
- Owner 該大寫，不加標點。
- 字型難看：Times New Roman。

Chapter 36 推薦函：Recommendations

寫推薦函，最重要的是：short and sweet, specific and concrete。不要寫廢話、客套話。推薦函格式同商業書信，請參考前章。推薦函，主要兩種：求職、申請學校。

Job recommendations

重點是工作。首先簡單說明如何認識申請人、認識多久：越久越好。推薦函焦點放在申請人一兩個特徵、成就。強調申請人的經驗、如何勝任、能力為何適合這分工作：connect the person to the job. 要具體，不可空泛。務必要校對！

右頁是基本範例可參考。

爲甚麼非黑筆簽名不可

黑筆簽名不只因為是傳統，而且黑墨難改，不褪色，容易影印。有些特殊情形，如電子文件列印簽名，對方要求藍筆，以確定是親筆簽名，不是電子簽名，但其餘仍以黑墨為宜。

Subject: T H Owen, MD, recommendation for Joe Blow
Ms Haggard, Manager
Haggard and Haggard Osteoarthritis Clinic

Dear Dr Haggard:
I am writing on behalf of Joseph "Joe" Blow, who is applying for the position of Clinic Manager at Haggard and Haggard.

Joe has worked for me for six years at Owen Orthopedic Clinic (2016 – 2022). He has a strong grasp of orthopedics, so he is able to communicate easily with our doctors and nurses, as well as to hire new staff. He has delineated each person's position and duties clearly, which greatly enhances the smooth operation of our Clinic. The budgets he has prepared for OOC have been practical and easy to manage, with careful attention to detail.

You may remember the ghastly bus crash on the 538 Freeway last April. Joe was an unsung hero of that event, coordinating efforts among several hospitals and clinics, ensuring that each patient got the best, most timely care. Tempers were high, but Joe kept everybody calm and focused. This accomplishment suffices as evidence of his ability.

Joe has decided to leave us, because his wife has a job in your state. I recommend him to you in full confidence that you will be as pleased with his work as we are.

Truly,
Thomas Hugh Owen, MD
General Manager
Owen Orthopedic Clinic
123-1234-1234 x 108
[Linkedin URL]
[OOC website]

July 22, 2022

❖Email

Subject line: 寫推薦人姓名、主旨
招呼、祝福同商業書信。內容兩三段就夠了。簡短明瞭：一段頂多五六行。
對方可能要求寄紙本副本。注意他們有沒有規定的格式等。

❖ 紙本

基本形式同商業書信。用公司、單位信箋。
寫給某某人：
Dear Dr Haggard:
Dear Human Resources Manager:
與其寫 To Whom it May Concern，不如不寫招呼。
內容同 email。
簽名，先祝福，空四行，打字寫姓名、頭銜；如果信箋未注明，加 email、Linkedin URL。

例如
Sincerely,

Bartholomew Oobleck
Manager
oobleck@yaminqoli.com
[Linkedin URL]

再提醒：簽名處，不可畫線；姓名、頭銜等後不加句點、逗點。用黑筆簽名。

School recommendations

申請大學部，通常要兩封推薦函；研究所要三封。
二〇一九年，一萬九千人申請 University of California at Los Angeles 大學部；九萬多人申請 University of California at Santa Barbara 大學部，University of California at San Diego 還更多。請自己算算，一個申請人兩封推薦函，總共多少封推薦函？美國一班研究所一年大約有兩百五十人申請，250 x 3 = 750，可憐的 Admissions Committee 必須看七百多封推薦函，面臨崩潰。

這告訴我們甚麼？長話短說！！

最好一頁寫完，不要到第二頁。要留空給推薦人單位信箋、抬頭、祝福、簽名，所以能寫的不多：一字千金。斟酌，縮減，再斟酌。不寫廢話！

美國的情形與臺灣一樣：請老師寫推薦函，很多老師說，Write it yourself and I'll sign it. 藉老師的口說你修過課程最大的收穫、障礙、成就、突破。

很多學生認為要寫的很誇張，以為沒把申請人寫成愛因斯坦的指導教授就申請不到學校。空洞的內容吸引不了對方。換角度想：你申請學校＝老師挑選學生。你當老師，願意教信口開河的學生嗎？

推薦函，一樣有線上的、紙本的。與商業書信、求職推薦函大同小異。線上推薦函，subject line 注明申請人姓名（護照上的）、就讀學校、申請系所、出生年月日。有人寫紙本推薦函，標明申請人全名、申請系所、出生年月日，這樣比較安全。切記，申請人多，收發室難免有誤，所以強調，最好註明申請人姓名、申請系所。可以寫在信封。

有的學校有標準格式，要注意。因為學校不一定願意接受另附信件。很多代辦中心遇到標準格式，貪圖自己方便，上面寫：See attached letter，將紙本推薦函釘上去。學校有格式，有他們的用意；這樣做，或許降低錄取機會：申請人那麼多，你不重視學校的要求，少你一個無所謂。英美人重視 follow the instructions。

開場，寫
Dear Professors:
Dear Admissions Committee:

知道對方姓名，最好不過。
現在總該知道不要寫 To Whom It May Concern 吧。

第一段寫申請人姓名、申請系所；申請人與推薦人的關係。看過很多學生寫 It is my great honor to teach 某某人；拜託，你算老幾，老師教你還「榮幸」！？看過太多這種句子：She is the most amazing student I have ever taught! 你認為老師真的會這樣寫嗎？

還有一個忌諱：不要寫 your esteemed institution 或 your prestigious institution：沒禮貌！學校有名字，寫出來。

第二段寫修課最大的成就、收穫、突破、挫折等。寫 He was my student. 沒啥意義， 可寫：He took Advanced Art Theory and Renaissance Influence on Flemish Painters under my instruction.

長官寫工作表現。無論誰寫，要具體，要清楚。看過太多這種句子：His senior project was very good. 可以透露一下他的題目嗎？ Good，是怎麼樣的個 good 法？ She participated in my research project. 可以透露一下研究課題、學生擔任的工作嗎？最後一段，說明該生念貴校，一定勝任之類的話。客套話，全免！

Graduate School of Maize Agronomy

University of Pumpkin Pie
123 Cornstarch Blvd, Comstock Bldg, 321 P
Pumpkin Pie, TN 12345

June 19, 2026

PhD Program in Detasseling
Corncob University
123 Nowhere Street
Peoria Il 61616
USA

RE: application of **Halus Msiaw**, born June 30, 2000

Dear Admissions Committee:

Halus Msiaw is applying to the PhD program in Corn Detasseling at Corncob University. He took my graduate level courses in Corn Pollination 506 and Heterosis and Blight 544.

Halus is a pleasant student to teach, and never afraid of responsibility or experimenting. He displayed his talent for innovation in manual detasseling, developing a special technique that increases efficiency while decreasing occupational injuries. This technique is now widely used throughout corn growing regions, and called the Halus Tweak.

I am confident that Halus has a solid theoretical foundation in Agricultural Statistics, Pedodiversity, and Agricultural Biotechnology to excel in his studies in the Detasseling PhD Program at Corncob University. I am sure you will enjoy teaching him as much as we did.

Sincerely,

用黑筆簽名
Malina Kukuruza
Professor

錯誤示範：

PhD Program in Detasseling
Corncob University
123 Nowhere Street
Peoria Il 61616
USA

To Whom It May Concern:

I am a teacher of Agronomy at Pumpkin Pie University , which was established since 1881. PPU has a large, pleasant campus in a scenic area of our state. I have taught at PPU for three years. Many courses and many students have been taught by me during these three years, and the students all give me top marks for my teaching. My Instagram account is followed by many celebrities and influencers. I have a huge number of followers. They all "like" the photos taken by me on my cellphone and posted on IG. Today I am honored to introduce the most incredible "genius" I have ever taught, Willie Maize, who is applying to your esteemed institution.

He was very attentive in class and took copious notes, so his pen ran out of ink often and he had to borrow pens from his classmagtes.He is always study in the library late at night when nobody was around. The midnight oil is burned by him as he stays up late at night studying while he wake s up early to go jogging. Jogging along the road ,dogs are always happy to see him. He is brilliant, outstanding, clever, innovative, diligent, industrious, proactive, productive, proficient, efficient, sufficient, and moreover, he is a "good" student. And delicious chocolate chip cookies are baked by 374 his mother. These are brought to class by him and given by him to other students so other students will be friends with him. And he is a team player. And he always wears green sock which go nicely with his yellow shoe. And he has a passion for his studying. You always find him in the cheering section whenever the PPU Tiddlywinks Team had a competition. They said that the only reason why they were able to win the county tiddlywinks championship was that they were so inspired by his cheering. He always carry a large vuvuzela that was brown and black color, which are our school colors, and it was blown by him so the players would be encouraged by him. From this you can see how much he loves PPU. There is no doubt in my mind that the path he has choose will be succeeded in by him .

In conclusion, Willie Maize is the most “amazing” student who has ever
entered into instruction under my auspices if you have any questions,
please feel to contact me.
Forever yours,

Po Tater,
Assistant Teaching Assistant.

承認，這封有點誇張，但是很多申請人寄出的推薦函類似這封。本猩看過很多推薦函寫，「他自己一個人在家很認真讀書。」老師怎麼會知道呢？請長話短說。

Chapter 37 履歷表：Writing a Resume that Works

公司徵才，收一堆履歷表，請問，讀者認為，一份履歷表他們看多久？

答案是：七秒左右。換言之，你只有七秒讓他們重視你。請等一下，看時鐘、手機，數數七秒。很短。所以，履歷表要搶眼，務必一頁寫完。

視覺效果，排版要俐落，一目瞭然。適當運用色彩。第 13 章討論過字型。從事哪一行？若從事會計、財經、飛機駕駛之類的行業，可以考慮 Times New Roman；其餘，本猩還是要推薦 Lexend Deca：易讀、大方、乾脆。字型大小 12 為妥。

履歷表形式多樣，所以本書不出範例。建議用英文搜尋 resume builder、resume template；中文雖有資料，良莠不齊，有的還是上世紀的老套、錯字橫行。仔細研究，選最適合自己的 builder 或 template。每次應徵，履歷表需微調；忌諱千篇一律，要衡量公司的狀況、需求，職位的特色等等。

履歷表基本要素，不外姓名聯絡方式；摘要、目標；工作經驗、成就；教育；專長；亦可加語言能力、出版、正當嗜好。通常不加大頭照、性別、出生年月日、婚姻狀況、身高體重。千萬不可打錯、拼錯字。

聯絡方式，email、電話、現住的都市、LinkedIn URL、其餘如 Behance、Dribble、GitHub、個人專業 blog 或網站。摘要，兩三句為限，超過就反效果。目標，對初入社會的鮮肉尤其重要；務實。

工作經驗、成就，限最重要、最大的；便利商店掌櫃、速食店燒漢堡，不必寫。寫：頭銜、職位；公司名號、地點、性質；職責、成就；年資經歷。工作成就，寫具體。

- I led a team of five people selling sweet potatoes, who all ardently worked assiduously and devoted great efforts to the success of our venture.
- Under my leadership, our 5 person sweet potato sales force exceeded our monthly goal by 31%, generating US$16,800 in sales in our first month.

語言能力，若英語、國語外，還會閩南語、客家語、上海話、廣東話，都可寫進去。職場未必用得到許多方言，但多語能力，特別在美國，讓人佩服。

EPILOGUE ▶ 結語

本書論寫作技巧，而最重要的是，心中有話需要說。紅樓夢的詩技巧好、陳詞美，很難看，無病呻吟：他們是為了寫詩而寫詩，胸中沒有丘壑，寫的詩技巧再老練，空洞無物，文學價值不高。

要傳達想法，技巧熟練，還是需要發自內心，而內心藏著啥？Robert Pirsig 說，You want to know how to paint a perfect painting? It's easy. Make yourself perfect and then just paint naturally.

但是我們都不完美，所以我們還是需要多多練習。希望讀者發現寫作多有趣，天下可以寫的題材實在太多！

寫給筆友也是好方法。可以上 reddit.com 尋筆友群組：r/penpals；三十歲以上的讀者可以到 r/penpalsover30。找筆友，可以上網搜尋 pen pal，也有 app 可以下載。Slowly、Ablo、Bottled、 Paltalk、HelloTalk，風評不錯，但本猩沒用過，所以不能擔保。不要透露太多個資，慢慢來。好吧，不說了，再來是讀者變作者的時刻！寫作愉悅！

致　謝

陳文南、林世華，有他們的鼓勵、支持，這本書才能完成。

太座鞭策與各方面的支援。

Thanks to Dr Bonnie Shaver-Troup for making the Lexend Deca font freely available for use.

我數十年來的學生，我們一起從錯誤中學習。

本書獻給所有英文寫作想進步的人。Study hard!

Appendix

附錄：1000 實用字彙

Appendix ▶ 附錄：1000 實用字彙

學英文，就是要背很多單字。要寫作，需要更多單字，而字須慎選。下列一千單字，都是常用字，就是撰文的工具。每字出簡易解釋，故意不細說，因為需要讀者咀嚼、認識每一個字。

VERBS

abbreviate 簡寫
abhor 厭惡
abort 終止
abridge 刪節
abrogate 廢除（命令）
abstain 戒除
accelerate 加速
accommodate 包容
accomplish 成就
accord 協
accost 招呼
achieve 成就
acknowledge 承認
acquiesce 默許
acquit 決議無罪
adhere 黏著
adjourn 散會
admit 承認；接納
adore 愛慕
affirm 承認
alienate 離間
alleviate 減輕
allocate 分配
allude 隱喻
alter 修改
ambush 埋伏
ameliorate 緩和
amplify 放大
annihilate 消滅
annoy 煩
annul 取消
appease 姑息、討好
appreciate 深入了解
apprehend 逮捕
articulate 闡明
ascend 登
assault 攻
assimilate 同化
assure 保證
attack 攻
attribute 歸功于
augment 彌補
avert 避免
balk 退卻
bandy 提出討論
befuddle 惑
begrudge 慳貪
belie 反駁
believe 信
belittle 扁
benefit 裨益
berate 罵
beseech 求
besiege 圍攻
bestow 賜
betray 背叛
bewitch 蠱惑
bicker 鬥嘴
blacklist 列入黑名單
blend 和
blossom 開花
bludgeon 棍打
blunder 犯錯
blurt 衝口而出
boost 提高
boycott 杯葛
bud 發蕾
burgeon 茂盛
cease 止
circumscribe 畫定範圍
circumvent 避開
clarify 澂清
cling 執著

clog 塞住
clutch 抓住
coax 引誘
coerce 逼
collide 撞
commit 投入，不能回首
compensate 彌補
comprehend 掌握，理解
concede 認錯
concoct 調配（半吊子）
condense 凝聚
confine 限
conflict 衝突
constrain 約束
contaminate 感染
contravene 違犯
contrive 設計（半吊子）
convert 轉換
corroborate 佐證
countenance 默許
counterfeit 偽造
crimp 壓成波紋；掣肘
crumble 碎
decoy 引誘
dedicate 奉獻
defer 讓；延後
defy 違抗
deliberate 沈思
delineate 畫出輪廓
demolish 毀
depend 依
deplete 耗
deplore 厭惡
deposit 存
deride 譏
descend 降
despise 厭惡
detain 拘留
detect 偵查
deter 挫敗
deteriorate 衰敗
detest 厭惡
detract 譭謗
differ 異
digress 離題
discern 分辨
discomfit 使不安
disperse 散
disseminate 傳播
divert 歧
doctor 動手腳
douse 灌
elucidate 闡明
elude 規避
embellish 加油添醋
emphasize 加強
entangle 糾纏
entertain 款待
entrust 委任
enunciate 咬字清晰
envelop 囊括
erupt 火山噴發
evade 逃避
evaluate 評估
evaporate 蒸發
exaggerate 誇張
exasperate 使人不耐煩
excavate 發掘
extort 勒索
extricate 解
fade 褪
fasten 固定
fester 潰爛
fetch 撿回
fidget 蠕蠕
flourish 揮；茂盛
foment 醞釀
forbid 禁
forestall 預防
forfeit 棄權
forge 鍛造；偽造
fracture 碎裂
fret 煩惱
fudge 矇混
gallop 馳騁
glitter 閃爍
glossary 詞彙
gnaw 啃
grind 磨
gripe 撈叨
grumble 碎碎念
guffaw 爆笑
gulp 嚥
hallucinate 幻想
halt 止

hindor 阻
hoodwink 蒙在鼓裏
hypnotize 催眠
idolize 崇拜
ignore 不理不睬
imitate 模仿
impact 撞擊
impede 阻擋
implore 求
imply 暗示
incarcerate 囚禁
inculcate 諄諄教誨
indoctrinate 灌輸教條
insinuate 暗示（陰險）
instigate 激發
intrude 闖
invade 侵
irk 討人厭
irritate 討人厭
kidnap 綁票
libel 譭謗（文字）
lionize 崇拜
loiter 逗留
lurk 匿伏
lynch 私刑
malign 譭謗
malinger 裝病
melt 融化
mobilize 動員
muffle 消音
mumble 咕噥
mutiny 叛變
mutter 咕噥
nauseate 噁心
nibble 蠶食
nip 咬（小口）
nudge 輕推
nurture 養
obstruct 阻
oscillate 搖擺
ostracize 放逐
parch 烤焦
parody 諷刺
peek 偷窺
perch 棲
perish 亡
pertain 關係到
pervade 滲透
placate 安撫
plot 謀亂；鋪航線
pluck 撥
plummet 驟降
plunder 掠
plunge 驟降
precede 走在前頭
prevail 反敗為勝
prevaricate 說謊
proceed 向前走
procrastinate 明天再寫好了
prod 推動
proliferate 繁殖
prosper 繁盛
provoke 無故惹事
quaff 牛飲
quail 畏懼
quake 震動
quell 敉平
quibble 抬槓
quiver 抖
ransack 翻箱倒櫃
ratify 通過（法案）
raze 拆
react 反應
rebuff 斷然拒絕
reconcile 化解衝突
recruit 招兵買馬
recuperate 康復
refrain 不做
reimburse 賠償
reiterate 重說
rejuvenate 回春
rely 依賴
remain 遺留
remark 說出
renew 重新辦理
repose 休息
rescind 廢除
resent 懷恨
resist 反抗
respond 回應
restrict 限制
retain 保留
retaliate 報復
retreat 逃命
retrieve 撿回

revere 崇敬
revoke 撤回
roam 遨遊
rove 遨遊
salvage 撈
scald 燙
scorch 烤焦
seduce 誘惑
select 選
shatter 碎
shiver 抖
shrink 縮
shudder 哆嗦
shun 排斥
sidestep 避開
skip 跳過
slander 譭謗（言語）
slip 滑
smolder 悶燒
smother 窒息
sparkle 閃耀
split 劈
squander 揮霍
stagger 蹣跚
stalk 跟蹤
stammer 口吃
stifle 窒息
stipulate 規定
strew 散
strive 賣力
stroll 散步
strut 闊步走
stun 震
stutter 口吃
stymie 阻
submerge 潛
suffice 足
suffocate 窒息
supersede 取代
suppress 壓抑
surge 湧
surround 圍
sustain 撐
swindle 詐
tamper 動手腳
thrive 旺盛
thwart 挫敗（計畫）
topple （由上）推倒
torment 折磨
trace 透描；追查
tremble 抖
trespass 闖入（它人土地）
trip 躓
triumph 勝
undermine 陷
undulate 蕩漾
unearth 發掘
unleash 釋放
urge 慫恿
vanish 不見了
vanquish 敗
vary 變
waffle 含糊其詞
wave 揮手
weave 織；蛇行
weigh 秤
withdraw 抽回
wither 枯萎

NOUNS

abode 住宅
abrasion 磨損
abuse 虐待
abyss 無底深淵
accomplice 共犯
acme 造極
acrophobia 懼高症
acumen 敏銳
addiction 癮
adulation 崇拜
advance 向前進，預支薪資
advancement 推廣
adventure 探險
adversary 敵
adversity 逆境
affection 感情
affidavit 宣誓書
affiliation 聯繫
affliction 苦楚
affluence 富裕
affront 冒犯
agenda 議程
agility 靈敏

alias 化名
alimony 贍養費
allegiance 忠
alloy 合金
allure 勾引
ally 盟友
altercation 爭吵
amateur 業餘者
ambiance 氛圍
ambition 志氣、野心
amnesia 失憶；健忘
amnesty 赦
anachronism 不合時代
ancestry 祖
anecdote 故事
anesthetic 麻醉
anguish 痛苦
animosity 敵意
anomaly 例外
anthology 選集
antidote 解藥
antipathy 反感
antiseptic 殺菌劑
anvil 鐵砧
apartheid 種族隔離
aplomb 沈著
apoplexy 中風
artillery 砲
assets 資產
associate 來往者
astigmatism 散光
attire 穿著
avalanche 雪崩
avarice 貪
barbarian 蠻
battery 電池；毆打；砲臺
beeline 直線
benefactor 恩人
betrothal 婚姻
bevy 群
bias 成見
binge 一陣酗酒
blasphemy 褻瀆神明
blemish 瑕疵
blight 枯萎
bliss 愉悅
blot 墨點
blowhard 吹牛者
bodyguard 保鑣
bog 籔
boulder 大石
braggart 自吹自擂者
breath 呼吸
cabal 朋黨
calamity 災
cant 虛偽的陳腔濫調
catalyst 催化劑
chagrin 懊惱
chasm 淵
chauvinism 盲目愛國
chisel 鑿
claustrophobia 幽閉恐懼症
clergy 神職人員
cliché 陳腔濫調
cliff 崖
clod 土塊
clot 血塊
cloudburst 陣雨
colander 濾盆
collage 撕紙畫
collusion 共謀
combat 短兵相接
commotion 喧嘩
commuter 通勤者
companion 伴侶
compassion 慈悲
component 組成的成分
compromise 讓步、妥協
connoisseur 鑑賞者
connotation 弦外之音
conspiracy 陰謀
consternation 惑
context 上下文
contortionist 軟骨術者
contraband 違禁品
conundrum 難題
cornucopia 聚寶盆
crony 共犯
crumb 碎屑
cupboard 櫥櫃
curfew 宵禁
curriculum 課程
dearth 缺

debacle 一敗塗地
deference 恭敬順從
deferment 延後
depression 低窪；憂鬱；經濟崩潰
descendant 後裔
dilemma 兩難
diplomat 外交人員
dispute 爭吵
dissent 抗議
dissident 抗議者
doctrine 教條
dogma 教條
dolt 笨蛋
dome 圓頂
dullard 笨蛋
egress 出口
elite 菁英
eloquence 辯才無礙
emblem 輝
enormity 滔天大罪
enmity 敵意
entrepreneur 企業家
epicenter 震央
equilibrium 沈穩
equivalent 相當
erudition 滿腹墨水
essence 精髓
eulogy 誄
euphemism 美其名
euthanasia 安樂死
exuberance 神彩奕奕
facsimile 摹本
fanatic 狂熱人
fatigue 疲憊
fault 錯；斷層
felon 重刑犯
fiasco 一敗塗地
flaw 瑕疵
fledgling 雛鳥
foliage 草叢
foundation 基
fraction 分數
fragment 碎片
fragrance 香
fraud 詐欺
friction 摩擦
fury 怒
garbage 廚餘
gem 寶石
gesture 手勢
gist 要旨
glance 見如駟之過隙
glimpse 見如驚鴻一瞥
glutton 貪吃鬼
gorilla 大猩猩；萬獸之靈
gravel 碎石
grouch 從不笑的人
guilt 罪惡
gulf 灣
gust 陣風
hail 冰雹
harangue 長篇怒罵訓話
havoc 亂
hearsay 傳聞
heresy 邪說
hinges 鉸鏈
hoax 騙你的啦
hostage 人質
hubris 狂妄自大
hypocrisy 虛假
hypocrite 口是心非的人
idiosyncrasy 個性的特質
idol 偶像
illusion 幻覺
impasse 僵局
incel 非自願獨身
incense 香
indolence 懶
insomnia 失眠
instinct 本能
insurrection 造反
intuition 直覺
invoice 發票
jargon 術語（負面）
labyrinth 迷宮
lava 熔岩
lay 信徒（區別于神父等）
lazybones 懶人，自己查
leash 牽狗的繩子
levity 不莊重的搞笑
livelihood 謀生之道
luddite 反科技進步的人
lumber 木材
luxury 奢迷

magma 岩漿
margin 頁邊
massacre 屠殺
mastermind 主腦
maverick 不合群之馬
mettle 骨氣
minimalism 極簡主義
mirage 海事辰樓
miser 守財奴
misery 痛苦
misogynist 厭惡女性者
moron 白癡 （不是在罵你）
mundane 入俗的，不超凡
nadir 最低點
nihilism 虛無主義
nomad 群遊的人
nuance 弦外之音
nuisance 討人厭的事
obsession 執著、放不下
omen 凶兆
optimism 樂觀
option 選項
ornament 裝飾
outskirts 郊區
parade 遊行
parasite 寄生
pariah 被排斥的人
passion 短暫的強烈情緒
patina 銀、銅鏽
peak 峰
pebble 小石
peccadillo 瑕疵
pedant 學究
peer 同儕
penchant 垂涎
pendulum 擺子
penury 窮
perjury 偽證
pessimism 悲觀
pest 害蟲
philanthropy 慈善
pinnacle 峰頂
pivot 樞
platitude 陳腔濫調
plead 求
plot 故事情節；陰謀
podium 講臺
posture 姿態
precipice 崖
predilection 嗜好
premise 前提
premises 工作場所
presentiment 預感
procession 隊伍
profanity #&*@!!
pulse 脈搏
qualm 心中不安
quandary 困境
quarrel 爭吵
quirk 怪僻
racket 吵鬧
raconteur 很會說故事的人
rage 怒
raid 突襲
ransom 贖金
reactionary 反動派
recession 經濟蕭條
recital 獨奏會；朗誦
rejoinder 反駁
repercussions 橫生的枝節
reputation 譽
retinue 扈從
retrospective 回顧
rift 裂
rostrum 講桌
rubbish 垃圾
rupture 破裂
scabbard 鞘
scoundrel 惡人
secular 入世
sedition 叛國
segment 片段、部分
sheath 鞘
silhouette 黑色輪廓
skit 短劇
sleet 霰
slowpoke 慢動作的人
slug 蛞蝓
slur 誹謗
somersault 翻跟斗
souvenir 旅遊紀念品
spear 矛

sponge 海綿
squid 烏賊
stable 馬廄
status 地位
stickler 恪守者
stigma 污點
straggler 跟不上者
sycophant 馬屁精
symbol 象徵
tadpole 蝌蚪
talon 鷹爪
tangent 切入線
terror 恐怖
thicket 草叢
thrift 儉
thunderstorm 雷雨
totem 守護神，祖靈
trash 垃圾
travesty 諷刺、鬧劇
treachery 陰險
trepidation 懼
trifle 雞毛蒜皮
trinket 廉價飾品
truce 停火
turbulence 亂
turmoil 亂
uproar 喧嘩
vagabond 流浪者
veneer 表面薄片
veneration 崇敬
verdict （法院）判決定讞
vestige 遺留的痕跡
vigil 守夜
vigor 精力
volcano 火山
wardrobe 衣櫃
warlock 覡
warlord 軍閥
warmonger 黷武者
whimsy 奇思妙想
wick 蠟燭蕊
yarn 羊毛線
zenith 天頂

ADJECTIVES

absolute 絕對
abysmal 無底爛
academic 學術
accessible 可通達
acquire 漸獲
acrimonious 刻薄
active 活
adamant 堅持
adhesive 黏
adjacent 鄰接
adroit 靈活
affable 友善
aggressive 愛攻
aghast 害怕如見鬼
ambiguous 模稜兩可
ambivalent 不置可否
amiable 友善
amiss 不對勁
anonymous 無名
antique 古董
antithetical 對立；不相容
anxious 焦慮
apprehensive 憂慮
apropos 適當
arbitrary 任意
arrogant 傲
askew 自己 google 一下
astonishing 令人目瞪口呆
asunder 裂
asymmetric 不對稱
atrocious 滔天大罪
audacious 恬不知恥
auspicious 吉
austere 嚴厲
authentic 真
avaricious 貪
awful 爛
awkward 尷尬
balmy 風和日麗
bankrupt 破產
bashful 害羞
becoming 讓某人更美
belated 遲
bellicose 好戰
belligerent 找碴
benevolent 善意
benign 善良

bereaved 守喪
berserk 抓狂
bigoted 偏見
bitter 苦
bizarre 詭異
bland 乏味
blasphemous 褻瀆神明
blatant 目無法紀
bleak 淒涼
blithe 傻乎乎的愉悅
bloated 吃完年夜飯
blunt 鈍
blurred 模糊
bogus 假
boisterous 調皮
bold 大膽
bombastic 誇誇其談
bumpy 顛簸
callous 無情
candid 坦率
casual 不正視
charismatic 魅力
coarse 粗
cognizant 認知
comprehensive 徹底
compulsive 情不自禁
concave 凹
conceited 自負
conciliatory 和解
condescending 傲慢
congested 堵
conspicuous 顯
contagious 傳染性
contemporary 當代
contentious 好爭
contrite 悔
convex 凸
copious 豐
covert 隱藏
cranky 吃錯藥，易怒
craven 孬種
critical 批評；臨界
crucial 關鍵
cruel 慘酷
cryptic 莫測
cumbersome 笨重不易搬動
cunning 狡猾
cursory 草率
dainty 纖巧
dashing 瀟灑
debonair 斯文風趣
delicate 易碎
derogatory 貶損
destitute 窮
discreet 謹慎
discrete 分離
disheveled 衣容不整
distraught 煩躁
diverse 分歧
docile 溫順
doctrinaire 墨守教條
dogmatic 墨守教條
dominant 主導
double 重複
double 請看前字
drab 無光無色
dreadful 可怕
drenched 濕透
drowsy 背單字的狀況
dubious 心懷疑問
ebullient 愉悅旺盛
edible 可吃
elated 樂昏了
emaciated 皮包骨
empirical 實證
energetic 精神抖擻
engrossed 全神貫注
enormous 大（如災難）
equivocal 模稜兩可
erratic 不穩
esoteric 玄奧
eternal 永
exempt 免除
exorbitant 敲竹槓
extant 仍存在
external 外在
extinct 絕種
far-fetched 離譜
far-flung 廣布
fatal 致命
feasible 可行
feeble 虛弱
feral 野
flamboyant 炫
flippant 輕佻

fragile 易碎
frantic 慌
fraudulent 詐欺
frigid 冰
frivolous 輕浮
frugal 儉
fulsome 讒媚
garish 俗麗
garrulous 囉唆
gaudy 絢麗
gaunt 皮包骨
generous 慷慨
glib 佞
gloomy 黯淡無光
glossy 光亮
grim 嚴肅
gullible 易騙
hapless 倒楣
haughty 驕傲
hollow 空虛
hospitable 好客
huge 巨
humble 謙虛
identical 一模一樣
idle 懶
illicit 不合法
immaculate 一塵不染
immense 廣闊
impartial 中立
imperial 皇帝的
impertinent 沒大沒小
implacable 無法息怒
impromptu 即興
impudent 沒大沒小
impulsive 衝動
inadequate 不足
inchoate 雛形；朦懂
incomprehensible 無法懂
incongruous 不和諧
incorrigible 無法改正
incredulous 無法相信
indigenous 本土
inevitable 無法避免
infamous 惡名昭彰
infectious 傳染
inferior 劣
infernal 天殺的
ingenious 天才
inquisitive 好奇
insufficient 不足
intellectual 智能（與智慧無關）
intentional 故意
internal 內
invincible 如金城湯池
invisible 隱
irrational 悖理
irrepressible 克制不住
irresponsible 不負責任
irrevocable 不可撤銷
jagged 崎嶇
jingoism 好戰的愛國
jovial 樂融融
jubilant 樂陶陶
latent 潛在
laudatory 讚美
lax 鬆弛；洛杉磯機場
lethal 致命
lethargic 懶洋洋
liable 有刑責；偏向
lucid 明暸
magnanimous 大方
malicious 惡意
malleable 可塑
meager 微不足道
meretricious 俗麗
meticulous 細心
mischievous 調皮
modest 謙
moribund 垂死
mortal 致命
nebulous 朦朧
negligent 疏忽
negligible 微不足道
nervous 緊張
neutral 中立
nonchalant 彷若無事人
notorious 惡名昭彰
oblivious （對周遭）冷漠
obscure 暗、不出名
obsequious 阿諛
obsolete 過期
obstinate 固執
obstreperous 吵鬧

obvious 明顯
odious 可惡
offhand 不經意
opaque 不透光
original 創新
ostentatious 誇耀
outgoing 外向
outrageous 令人怒懟
patriotic 愛國
perfunctory 搪塞
perpendicular 垂直
petulant 嘟嘴
picky 挑剔
polite 客氣
plastic 可塑造
plump 略胖
pompous 自認不凡
ponderous 笨重
precarious 累卵
precocious 未長已熟
precursory 草率
prejudiced 成見
preposterous 荒謬
pretentious 做作
pristine 純潔
prodigious 龐大
profound 深邃
pudgy 胖嘟嘟
punctilious 拘泥形式
quixotic 不切實務
random 亂碼
recalcitrant 不順從
reciprocal 互惠
reckless 莽撞
recondite 深奧
reluctant 不情願
remarkable 特殊
reminiscent 喚起回憶
renowned 著名
repulsive 醜八怪
resigned 認命
resilient 康復力強
robust 強壯
rotund 圓滾滾
sacred 神聖
scarce 稀少
scared 害怕
scarred 有疤痕
scathing 傷人
scrawny 皮包骨
secluded 隱密
secure 安全
self-centered 自我中心
sheer 如絕壁
shrewd 精明
simultaneous 同時
skeptical 相信本猩嗎
slack 鬆弛
sluggish 遲緩
smart 聰明（與智慧無關）
soggy 濕
spontaneous 自發
sporadic 間歇
staunch 堅決
steadfast 堅決
stooped 佝僂
strident 刺耳
subtle 微妙
superfluous 冗
superior 優
susceptible 易感染、影響
symmetrical 對稱
tangible 具體
temporary 暫
tender 嫩
tepid 不冷不熱
thrifty 儉
tragic 悲傷
tranquil 寧
transitory 無常
translucent 透光
transparent 透明
trenchant 深刻
trivial 區區
ubiquitous 遍在
uncouth 沒禮貌
unfounded 無稽之談
unscathed 毫髮無傷
urbane 素養優
urgent 緊急
vacant 虛
vacuous 腦虛面呆
vague 這也講不清楚
vain 虛榮

vast 遼闊
venomous （咬人）有毒
verbose 囉唆
verdant 蔥綠
versatile 多能、能適應
vicious 凶猛
vile 卑劣
vindictive 必報仇
violent 暴力
volatile 易變
vulgar 俗
wealthy 富
weird 詭異
wise 智慧

你絕對用得上的英文寫作：高級商務．升學．托福多益．求職，全方位生活應用指南

國家圖書館出版品預行編目（CIP）資料

你絕對用得上的英文寫作：高級商務．升學．托福多益．求職，全方位生活應用指南 / 陶維極 G B Talovich 著 . -- 初版 . -- 臺北市：風和文創事業有限公司 , 2022.8
面； 公分
ISBN 978-626-95383-8-6 (平裝)
1.CST: 英語 2.CST: 寫作法
805.17 111009379

作者 陶維極 G B Talovich
總經理暨總編輯 李亦榛
特助 鄭澤琪
主編 張艾湘
封面設計 古杰
版面構成與編排 楊佩菱

出版公司 風和文創事業有限公司
地址 台北市大安區光復南路 692 巷 24 號 1 樓
電話 02-2755-0888
傳真 02-2700-7373
Email sh240@sweethometw.com
網址 www.sweethometw.com.tw

IESG 台灣版 SH 美化家庭出版授權方
凌速姐妹 (集團) 有限公司
In Express-Sisters Group Limited

公司地址 香港九龍荔枝角長沙灣道 883 號億利工業中心 3 樓 12-15 室
董事總經理 梁中本
Email cp.leung@iesg.com.hk
網址 www.iesg.com.hk

總經銷 聯合發行股份有限公司
地　址 新北市新店區寶橋路 235 巷 6 弄 6 號 2 樓
電　話 02-29178022

印製 兆騰印刷設計有限公司
定價 新台幣 380 元
出版日期 2022 年 8 月初版一刷